John Berger

Pig Earth

John Berger was born in London in 1926. He is well known for his novels and stories as well as for his works of nonfiction, including several volumes of art criticism. His first novel, *A Painter of Our Time*, was published in 1958, and since then his books have included the novel *G.*, which won the Booker Prize in 1972.

With *Lilac and Flag* (1990), Berger completed his peasant trilogy *Into Their Labours*, which also includes *Pig Earth* (1979) and *Once in Europa* (1987). His volumes of essays include *Keeping a Rendezvous* (1991), *The Sense of Sight* (1985), *Ways of Seeing* (1972), and *Selected Essays* (2001).

In 1962 Berger left Britain permanently, and he now lives in a small village in the French Alps.

INTERNATIONAL

The works of John Berger

PIG EARTH (first book
of the INTO THEIR LABOURS trilogy)
ONCE IN EUROPA (second book of the trilogy)
LILAC AND FLAG (third book of the trilogy)
A PAINTER OF OUR TIME
PERMANENT RED
THE FOOT OF CLIVE
CORKER'S FREEDOM
A FORTUNATE MAN
ART AND REVOLUTION
THE MOMENT OF CUBISM AND OTHER ESSAYS
THE LOOK OF THINGS: SELECTED ESSAYS AND ARTICLES
WAYS OF SEEING
ANOTHER WAY OF TELLING
A SEVENTH MAN
G.
ABOUT LOOKING
AND OUR FACES, MY HEART, BRIEF AS PHOTOS
THE SENSE OF SIGHT
THE SUCCESS AND FAILURE OF PICASSO
KEEPING A RENDEZVOUS
TO THE WEDDING
KING
PHOTOCOPIES
THE SHAPE OF A POCKET
SELECTED ESSAYS

PIG

EARTH

JOHN BERGER

PIG
EARTH

VINTAGE INTERNATIONAL
VINTAGE BOOKS
A DIVISION OF RANDOM HOUSE, INC.
NEW YORK

FIRST VINTAGE INTERNATIONAL EDITION, NOVEMBER 1992

Copyright © 1979 by John Berger

All rights reserved under International and Pan-American Copyright Conventions.
Published in the United States by Vintage Books, a division of Random House, Inc.,
New York, and distributed in Canada by Random House of Canada Limited, Toronto.
Originally published in Great Britain by Writers and Readers Publishing Cooperative,
in 1979 and in the United States by Pantheon Books, a division of Random House,
Inc., New York, in 1980.

Library of Congress Cataloging-in-Publication Data
Berger, John.
  Pig earth / John Berger.
    p.   cm.
  Originally published: New York: Pantheon, 1979.
  ISBN 978-0-679-73715-5 (pbk.)
    1. Country Life—France—Alps, French—Fiction.   2. Peasantry—
France—Alps, French—Fiction.   3. Alps, French (France)—Fiction.
I. Title.
[PR6052.E564P54   1992]
823'.914—dc20   92-50074   CIP

Manufactured in the United States of America
20 19 18

"Others have laboured and ye are entered into their labours."

ST JOHN 4-38

This book is dedicated to five friends who have taught us:

Théophile Jorat
Angeline Coudurier
André Coudurier
Théophile Gay
Marie Raymond

to the friends who have helped us learn:

Raymond Berthier, Luc and Marie-Thérese Bertrand, Gervais and Mélina Besson, Jean-Paul Besson, Denis Besson, Michel Besson, Gérard Besson, Christian Besson, Marius Chavanne, Roger and Noelle Coudurier, Michel Coudurier, La Doxie, Régis Duret, Gaston Forrestier, Marguerite Gay, Noel and Hélène Gay, Marcelle Gay, Jeanne Jorat, Armand Jorat, Daniel and Yvette Jorat, Norbert Jorat, Maurice and Claire Jorat, François and Germaine Malgrand, Francis and Joelle Malgrand. Marcel Nicoud, André Perret, Yves and Babette Peter, Jean-Marie and Josephine Pittet, Roger and Rolande Pittet, Bernadette Pittet, François Ramel, Francois and Léonie Raymond, Basil Raymond, Guy and Anne-Marie Roux, Le Violon, Walter

and to Beverly with whom I learn.

Introduction

"The earth shows up those of value and those who are good for nothing." A peasant judgement quoted by Jean Pierre Vernant in *Mythe et Pensée Chez les Grecs*. (Vol. 2. Paris 1971)

"The peasantry consists of small agricultural producers who with the help of simple equipment and the labour of their families produce mainly for their own consumption and for the fulfillment of obligations to the holders of political and economic power." Theodor Shanin. *Peasants and Peasant Societies*. (London 1976)

PEASANT LIFE is a life committed completely to survival. Perhaps this is the only characteristic fully shared by peasants everywhere. Their implements, their crops, their earth, their masters may be different, but whether they labour within a capitalist society, a feudal one or others which cannot be so easily defined, whether they grow rice in Java, wheat in Scandinavia or maize in South America, whatever the differences of climate, religion and social history, the peasantry everywhere can be defined as a class of survivors. For a century and a half now the tenacious ability of peasants to survive has confounded administrators and theorists. Today it can still be said that the majority in the world are peasants. Yet this fact masks a more significant one. For the first time ever it is possible that the class of survivors may not survive. Within a century there may be no more peasants. In Western Europe, if the plans work out as the economic planners have foreseen, there will be no more peasants within twenty-five years.

Until recently, the peasant economy was always an economy within an economy. This is what has enabled it to survive global transformations of the larger economy—feudal, capitalist, even socialist. With these transformations the peasant's mode of struggle for survival often altered but the decisive changes were wrought in the methods used for extracting a surplus from him: compulsory labour services, tithes, rents, taxes, sharecropping, interests on loans, production norms, etc.

Unlike any other working and exploited class, the peasantry has always supported itself and this made it, to some degree, a class apart. In so far as it produced the necessary surplus, it was integrated into the historical economic-cultural system. In so far as it supported itself, it was on the frontier of that system. And I think one can say this, even where and when peasants make up the majority of the population.

If one thinks of the hierarchical structure of feudal or Asian societies as being roughly pyramidal, the peasantry were on the base frontier of the triangle. This meant, as with all frontier populations, that the political and social system offered them the minimum of protection. For this they had to look to themselves— within the village community and the extended family. They maintained or developed their own unwritten laws and codes of behaviour, their own rituals and beliefs, their own orally transmitted body of wisdom and knowledge, their own medicine, their own techniques and sometimes their own language. It would be wrong to suppose that all this constituted an independent culture, unaffected by the dominant one and by its economic, social or technical developments. Peasant life did not stay exactly the same throughout the centuries, but the priorities and values of peasants (their strategy for survival) were embedded in a tradition which outlasted any tradition in the rest of society. The undeclared relation of this peasant tradition, at any given moment, to the dominant class culture was often heretical and subversive. "Don't run away from anything," says the Russian peasant proverb, "but don't do anything." The peasant's universal reputation for cunning is a recognition of this secretive and subversive tendency.

No class has been or is more economically conscious than the peasantry. Economics consciously determines or influences every ordinary decision which a peasant takes. But his economics are not those of the merchant, nor those of bourgeois or Marxist political economy. The man who wrote with most understanding about lived peasant economics was the Russian agronomist Chayanov. Anyone who wishes to understand the peasant should, among other things, go back to Chayanov.

The peasant did not conceive of what was extracted from him as a surplus. One might argue that the politically unconscious proletarian is equally unaware of the surplus value he creates for his employer, yet the comparison is misleading—for the worker, working for wages in a money economy, can be easily deceived about the value of what he produces, whereas the peasant's *economic* relation to the rest of society was always transparent. His family produced or tried to produce what they needed to live on, and he saw part of this produce, the result of his family's labour, being appropriated by those who had not laboured. The peasant was perfectly aware of what was being extracted from him, yet he did not think of this as a surplus for two reasons, the first material and the second epistemological. 1) It was not a surplus because his family needs had not already been assured. 2) A surplus is an end product, the result of a long-completed process of working and of meeting requirements. To the peasant, however, his enforced social obligations assumed the form of a *preliminary obstacle*. The obstacle was often insurmountable. But it was on the other side of it that the other half of the peasant economy operated, whereby his family worked the land to assure its own needs.

A peasant might think of his imposed obligations as a natural duty, or as some inevitable injustice, but in either case they were something which had to be endured *before* the struggle for survival opened. He had first to work for his masters, later for himself. Even if he were sharecropping, the master's share came *before* the basic needs of his family. If the work were not too light in the face of the almost unimaginable burden of labour placed on the peasant, one might say that his enforced obligations assumed the form of a permanent handicap. It was *despite this* that the family had to open the already uneven struggle with nature to gain by their own work their own subsistence.

Thus the peasant had to survive the permanent handicap of

having a "surplus" taken from him; he had to survive, in the subsistence half of his economy, all the hazards of agriculture—bad seasons, storms, droughts, floods, pests, accidents, impoverished soil, animal and plant diseases, crop failures; and furthermore, at the base frontier, with the minimum of protection, he had to survive social, political and natural catastrophes—wars, plagues, brigands, fire, pillaging, etc.

The word *survivor* has two meanings. It denotes somebody who has survived an ordeal. And it also denotes a person who has continued to live when others disappeared or perished. It is in this second sense that I am using the word in relation to the peasantry. Peasants were those who remained working, as distinct from the many who died young, emigrated or became paupers. At certain periods those who survived were certainly a *minority*. Demographic statistics give some idea of the dimensions of the disasters. The population of France in 1320 was seventeen million. A little over a century later it was eight million. By 1550 it had climbed to twenty million. Forty years later it fell to eighteen million.

In 1789 the population was twenty-seven million, of whom twenty-two million were rural. The revolution and the scientific progress of the nineteenth century offered the peasant land and physical protection such as he had not known before; at the same time they exposed him to capital and the market economy; by 1848 the great peasant exodus to the cities had begun and by 1900 there were only eight million French peasants. The deserted village has probably almost always been—and certainly is again today—a feature of the countryside: it represents a site of no survivors.

A comparison with the proletariat in the early stages of the industrial revolution may clarify what I mean by a class of survivors. The working and living conditions of the early proletariat condemned millions to early death or disabling illness. Yet the class as a whole, its numbers, its capacity, its power, was growing. It was a class engaged in, and submitting to, a process of continual transformation and increase. It was not the victims of its ordeals who determined its essential class character, as in a class of survivors, but rather its demands and those who fought for them.

From the eighteenth century onwards populations all over the world mounted, at first slowly and later dramatically. Yet for the peasantry this general experience of a new security of life could not overlay its class memory of earlier centuries, because the new conditions, including those brought about by improved agricultural techniques, entailed new threats: the large-scale commercialisation and colonialisation of agriculture, the inadequacy of ever smaller plots of land to support entire families, hence large-scale emigration to the cities where the sons and daughters of peasants were absorbed into another class.

The nineteenth-century peasantry was still a class of survivors, with the difference that those who disappeared were no longer those who ran away or who died as a result of famine and disease, but those who were forced to abandon the village and become wage earners. One should add that under these new conditions a few peasants became rich, but in doing so they also ceased, within a generation or two, to be peasants.

To say that peasants are a class of survivors may seem to confirm what the cities with their habitual arrogance have always said about peasants—that they are backward, a relic of the past. Peasants themselves, however, do not share the view of time implicit in such a judgement.

Inexhaustibly committed to wresting a life from the earth, bound to the present of endless work, the peasant nevertheless sees life as an interlude. This is confirmed by his daily familiarity with the cycle of birth, life and death. Such a view may predispose him to religion, yet religion is not at the origin of his attitude and, anyway, the religion of peasants has never fully corresponded with the religion of rulers and priests.

The peasant sees life as an interlude because of the dual contrary movement through time of his thoughts and feelings which in turn derives from the dual nature of the peasant economy. His dream is to return to a life that is not handicapped. His determination is to hand on the means of survival (if possible made more secure, compared to what he inherited) to his children. His ideals are located in the past; his obligations are to the future, which he himself will not live to see. After his death he will not be transported into the future—his notion of immortality is different: he will return to the past.

These two movements, towards the past and the future, are not as contrary as they might first appear because basically the peasant has a cyclic view of time. The two movements are different ways of going round a circle. He accepts the sequence of centuries without making that sequence absolute. Those who have a unilinear view of time cannot come to terms with the idea of cyclic time: it creates a moral vertigo since all their morality is based on cause and effect. Those who have a cyclic view of time are easily able to accept the convention of historic time, which is simply the trace of the turning wheel.

The peasant imagines an unhandicapped life, a life in which he is not first forced to produce a surplus before feeding himself and his family, as a primal state of being which existed before the advent of injustice. Food is man's first need. Peasants work on the land to produce food to feed themselves. Yet they are forced to feed others first, often at the price of going hungry themselves. They see the grain in the fields which they have worked and harvested—on their own land or on the landowner's—being taken away to feed others, or to be sold for the profit of others. However much a bad harvest is considered an act of God, however much the master/landowner is considered a natural master, whatever ideological explanations are given, the basic fact is clear: they who can feed themselves are instead being forced to feed others. Such an injustice, the peasant reasons, cannot always have existed, so he assumes a just world at the beginning. At the beginning a primary state of justice towards the primary work of satisfying man's primary need. All spontaneous peasant revolts have had the aim of resurrecting a just and egalitarian peasant society.

This dream is not the usual version of the dream of paradise. Paradise, as we now understand it, was surely the invention of a relatively leisured class. In the peasant's dream, work is still necessary. Work is the condition for equality. Both the bourgeois and Marxist ideals of equality presume a world of plenty; they demand equal rights for all before a cornucopia, a cornucopia to be constructed by science and the advancement of knowledge. What the two understand by equal rights is of course very different. The peasant ideal of equality recognises a world of scarcity, and its promise is for mutual fraternal aid in struggling against this scarcity and a just sharing of what the work produces. Closely connected with the peasant's recognition, as a survivor, of scarcity is his recognition of man's relative ignorance. He may admire knowledge and the fruits of knowledge but he never supposes that the advance of knowledge reduces the extent of the unknown. This non-antagonistic relation between the unknown and knowing explains why some of his knowledge is accommodated in what, from the outside, is defined as superstition and magic. Nothing in his experience encourages him to believe in final causes, precisely because his experience is so wide. The unknown can only be eliminated within the limits of a laboratory experiment. Those limits seem to him to be naïve.

Opposing the movement of the peasant's thoughts and feelings about a justice in the past are other thoughts and feelings directed towards the survival of his children in the future. Most of the time the latter are stronger and more conscious. The two movements balance each other only in so far as together they convince him that the interlude of the present cannot be judged in its own terms; morally it is judged in relation to the past, materially it is judged in relation to the future. Strictly speaking, nobody is less opportunist (taking the immediate opportunity regardless) than the peasant.

How do peasants think or feel about the future? Because their work involves intervening in or aiding an organic process most of their actions are future-oriented. The planting of a tree is an obvious example, but so, equally, is the milking of a cow: the milk is for cheese or butter. Everything they do is anticipatory— and therefore never finished. They envisage this future, to which they are forced to pledge their actions, as a series of ambushes. Ambushes of risks and dangers. The most likely future risk, until recently, was hunger. The fundamental contradiction of the peasant's situation, the result of the dual nature of the peasant economy, was that they who produced the food were the most likely to starve. A class of survivors cannot afford to believe in an arrival point of assured security or well-being. The only, but great, future hope is survival. This is why the dead do better to return to the past where they are no longer subject to risk.

The future path through future ambushes is a continuation of the old path by which the survivors from the past have come. The image of a path is apt because it is by following a path, created and maintained by generations of walking feet, that some of the dangers of the surrounding forests or mountains or marshes may be avoided. The path is tradition handed down by instructions, example and commentary. To a peasant the future is this future narrow path across an indeterminate expanse of known and unknown risks. When peasants cooperate to fight an outside force, and the impulse to do this is always defensive, they adopt a guerrilla strategy—which is precisely a network of narrow paths across an indeterminate hostile environment.

The peasant view of human destiny, such as I am outlining, was not, until the advent of modern history, essentially different from the view of other classes. One has only to think of the poems of Chaucer, Villon, Dante; in all of them Death, whom nobody can escape, is the surrogate for a generalized sense of uncertainty and menace in face of the future.

Modern history begins—at different moments in different places—with the principle of progress as both the aim and motor of history. This principle was born with the bourgeoisie as an ascendant class, and has been taken over by all modern theories of revolution. The twentieth-century struggle between capitalism and socialism is, at an ideological level, a fight about the content of progress. Today within the developed world the initiative of this struggle lies, at least temporarily, in the hands of capitalism which argues that socialism produces backwardness. In the underdeveloped world the "progress" of capitalism is discredited.

Cultures of progress envisage future expansion. They are forward-looking because the future offers ever larger hopes. At their most heroic these hopes dwarf Death (*La Rivoluzione o la Morte!*). At their most trivial they ignore it (consumerism). The future is envisaged as the opposite of what classical perspective does to a road. Instead of appearing to become ever narrower as it recedes into the distance, it becomes ever wider.

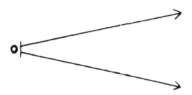

A culture of survival envisages the future as a sequence of repeated acts for survival. Each act pushes a thread through the eye of a needle and the thread is tradition. No overall increase is envisaged.

If now, comparing the two types of culture, we consider their view of the past as well as the future, we see that they are mirror opposites of one another.

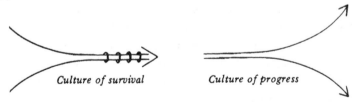

Culture of survival   *Culture of progress*

This may help to explain why an experience within a culture of survival can have the opposite *significance* to the comparable experience within a culture of progress. Let us take, as a key example, the much proclaimed conservatism of the peasantry, their resistance to change; the whole complex of attitudes and reactions which often (not invariably) allows a peasantry to be counted as a force for the right wing.

First, we must note that the counting is done by the cities, according to an historical scenario opposing left to right, which belongs to a culture of progress. The peasant refuses that scenario, and he is not stupid to do so, for the scenario, whether the left or right win, envisages his disappearance. His conditions of living, the degree of his exploitation and his suffering may be desperate, but he cannot contemplate the disappearance of what gives meaning to everything he knows, which is, precisely, his will to survive. No worker is ever in that position, for what gives meaning to his life is either the revolutionary hope of transforming it, or money, which is received in exchange against his life as a wage earner, to be spent in his "true life" as a consumer.

Any transformation of which the peasant dreams involves his re-becoming "the peasant" he once was. The worker's political dream is to transform everything which up to now has condemned him to be a worker. This is one reason why an alliance between workers and peasants can only be maintained if it is for a specific aim (the defeat of a foreign enemy, the expropriation of large landowners) to which both parties are agreed. No general alliance is normally possible.

To understand the significance of peasant conservatism related to the sum of peasant experience, we need to examine the idea of change with a different optic. It is an historical commonplace that change, questioning, experiment, flourished in the cities and emanated outwards from them. What is often overlooked is the character of everyday urban life which allowed for such an interest in research. The city offered to its citizens comparative security, continuity, permanence. The degree offered depended upon the class of the citizen, but compared to life in a village, all citizens benefited from a certain protection.

There was heating to counteract changes of temperature, lighting to lessen the difference between night and day, transport to reduce distances, relative comfort to compensate for fatigue; there were walls and other defences against attack, there was effective law, there were almshouses and charities for the sick and aged, there were libraries of permanent written knowledge, there was a wide range of services—from bakers and butchers through mechanics and builders to doctors and surgeons—to be called upon whenever a need threatened to disrupt the customary flow of life, there were conventions of social behaviour which strangers were obliged to accept (when in Rome . . .), there were buildings designed as promises of, and monuments to, continuity.

During the last two centuries, as urban theories and doctrines of change have become more and more vehement, the degree and efficacy of such everyday protection has correspondingly increased. Recently the insulation of the citizen has become so total that it has become suffocating. He lives alone in a serviced limbo— hence his newly-awakened, but necessarily naïve, interest in the countryside.

By contrast the peasant is unprotected. Each day a peasant experiences more change more closely than any other class. Some of these changes, like those of the seasons or like the process of ageing and failing energy, are foreseeable; many—like the weather from one day to the next, like a cow choking to death on a potato, like lightning, like rains which come too early or too late, like fog that kills the blossom, like the continually evolving demands of those who extract the surplus, like an epidemic, like locusts—are unpredictable.

In fact the peasant's experience of change is more intense than any list, however long and comprehensive, could ever suggest. For two reasons. First, his capacity for observation. Scarcely anything changes in a peasant's entourage, from the clouds to the tail feathers of a cock, without his noticing and interpreting it in terms of the future. His active observation never ceases and so he is continually recording and reflecting upon changes. Secondly, his economic situation. This is usually such that even a slight change for the worse—a harvest which yields twenty-five per cent less than the previous year, a fall in the market price of the harvest produce, an unexpected expense—can have disastrous or near-disastrous consequences. His observation does not allow the slightest sign of change to pass unnoticed, and his debt magnifies the real or imagined threat of a great part of what he observes.

Peasants live with change hourly, daily, yearly, from generation to generation. There is scarcely a constant given to their lives except the constant necessity of work. Around this work and its seasons they themselves create rituals, routines and habits in order to wrest some meaning and continuity from a cycle of remorseless change: a cycle which is in part natural and in part the result of the ceaseless turning of the millstone of the economy within which they live.

The very great variety of these routines and rituals which attach themselves to work and to the different phases of a working life (birth, marriage, death) are the peasant's own protection against a state of continual flux. Work routines are traditional and cyclic— they repeat themselves each year, and sometimes each day. Their tradition is retained because it appears to assure the best chance of the work's success, but also because, in repeating the same routine, in doing the same thing in the same way as his father or his neighbour's father, the peasant assumes a continuity for himself and thus consciously experiences his own survival.

The repetition, however, is essentially and only formal. A work routine for a peasant is very different from most urban work routines. Each time a peasant does the same job there are elements in it which have changed. The peasant is continually improvising. His faithfulness to tradition is never more than approximate. The traditional routine determines the ritual of the job: its content, like everything else he knows, is subject to change.

When a peasant resists the introduction of a new technique or method of working, it is not because he cannot see its possible advantages—his conservatism is neither blind nor lazy—but because he believes that these advantages cannot, by the nature of things, be guaranteed, and that, should they fail, he will then be cut off alone and isolated from the routine of survival. (Those working with peasants for improved production should take this into account. A peasant's ingenuity makes him open to change, his imagination demands continuity. Urban appeals for change are usually made on the opposite basis: ignoring ingenuity, which tends to disappear with the extreme division of labour, they promise the imagination a new life.)

Peasant conservatism, within the context of peasant experience, has nothing in common with the conservatism of a privileged ruling class or the conservatism of a sycophantic petty-bourgeoisie. The first is an attempt, however vain, to make their privileges absolute; the second is a way of siding with the powerful in exchange for a little delegated power over other classes. Peasant conservatism scarcely defends any privilege. Which is one reason why, much to the surprise of urban political and social theorists, small peasants have so often rallied to the defence of richer peasants. It is a conservatism not of power but of meaning. It represents a depository (a granary) of meaning preserved from lives and generations threatened by continual and inexorable change.

Many other peasant attitudes are frequently misunderstood or understood in an exactly opposite sense—as the diagram of the mirror-image has already suggested. For example, peasants are thought to be money-minded whereas, in fact, the behaviour which gives rise to this idea derives from a profound suspicion of money. For example, peasants are said to be unforgiving, yet this trait, in so far as it is true, is the result of the belief that life without justice becomes meaningless. It is rare for any peasant to die unforgiven.

We must now ask this question: What is the contemporary relation between peasants and the world economic system of which they form part? Or, to put this question in terms of our consideration of peasant experience: What significance can this experience have today in a global context?

Agriculture does not necessarily require peasants. The British peasantry was destroyed (except in certain areas of Ireland and Scotland) well over a century ago. In the USA there have been no peasants in modern history because the rate of economic development based on monetary exchange was too rapid and too total. In France 150,000 peasants now leave the land every year. The economic planners of the EEC envisage the systematic elimination of the peasant by the end of the century. For short-term political reasons, they do not use the word *elimination* but the word *modernisation*. Modernisation entails the disappearance of the small peasants (the majority) and the transformation of the remaining minority into totally different social and economic beings. The capital outlay for intensive mechanisation and chemicalisation, the necessary size of the farm exclusively producing for the market, the specialisation of produce by area, all mean that the peasant family ceases to be a productive and consuming unit, and that, instead, the peasant becomes the dependent of the interests which both finance him and buy from him. The economic pressure on which such a plan depends is supplied by the falling market value of agricultural produce. In France today the buying power of the price of one sack of wheat is three times less than it was fifty years ago. The ideological persuasion is supplied by all the promises of consumerism. An intact peasantry was the only class with an in-built resistance to consumerism. When a peasantry is dispersed, markets are enlarged.

In much of the Third World the systems of land tenure (in large parts of Latin America one per cent of landowners own sixty per cent of the farm land, and one hundred per cent of the best land), the imposition of monocultures for the benefit of corporate capitalism, the marginalisation of subsistence farming, and, only because of these other factors, the mounting population, cause more and more peasants to be reduced to such a degree of absolute poverty that, without land or seed or hope, they lose all previous social identity. Many of these ex-peasants make for the cities where they form a millionfold mass such as has never existed before, a mass of static vagrants, a mass of unemployed attendants: attendants in the sense that they wait in the shanty towns, cut off from the past, excluded from the benefits of progress, abandoned by tradition, serving nothing.

Engels and most early-twentieth-century Marxists foresaw the disappearance of the peasant in face of the greater profitability of capitalist agriculture. The capitalist mode of production would do away with small peasant production "as a steam engine smashes a wheelbarrow." Such prophecies underestimated the resilience of the peasant economy and overestimated the attraction of agriculture for capital. On the one hand, the peasant family could survive without profitability (cost accounting was inapplicable to the peasant economy); and on the other hand, for capital, land, unlike other commodities, is not infinitely reproduceable, and investment in agricultural production finally meets a constraint and yields decreasing returns.

The peasant has survived far longer than was predicted. But within the last forty years monopoly capital, through its multinational corporations, has created the new highly profitable structure of agribusiness whereby it controls, not necessarily the production, but the market for agricultural inputs and outputs and the processing, packaging and selling of every kind of foodstuff. The penetration of this market into all corners of the globe is eliminating the peasant. In the developed countries by more or less planned conversion; in the underdeveloped countries catastrophically. Previously cities were dependent on the countryside for their food, peasants being forced, in one way or another, to part with their so-called surplus. Soon the world countryside may be dependent on the cities even for the food its own rural population requires. When and if this happens, peasants will have ceased to exist.

During the same period of the last forty years, in other parts of the Third World—China, Cuba, Vietnam, Cambodia, Algeria—revolutions have been made by peasants, and in their name. It is too soon to know what kind of transformation of the peasant experience these revolutions will achieve, and how far their governments can or cannot maintain a different set of priorities to those imposed by the world market of capitalism.

It must follow from what I have already said that nobody can reasonably argue for the preservation and maintenance of the traditional peasant way of life. To do so is to argue that peasants should continue to be exploited, and that they should lead lives in which the burden of physical work is often devastating and always oppressive. As soon as one accepts that peasants are a class of survivors—in the sense in which I have defined the term—any idealisation of their way of life becomes impossible. In a just world such a class would no longer exist.

Yet to dismiss peasant experience as belonging only to the past, as having no relevance to modern life, to imagine that the thousands of years of peasant culture leave no heritage for the future—simply because it was seldom embodied in lasting objects—to continue to maintain, as has been maintained for centuries, that peasant experience is marginal to civilisation, is to deny the value of too much history and too many lives. No line of exclusion can be drawn across history in that manner, as if it were a line across a closed account.

The point can be made more precisely. The remarkable continuity of peasant experience and the peasant view of the world acquires, as it is threatened with extinction, an unprecedented and unexpected urgency. It is not only the future of peasants which is now involved in this continuity. The forces which in most parts of the world are today eliminating or destroying the peasantry represent the contradiction of most of the hopes once contained in the principle of historical progress. Productivity is not reducing scarcity. The dissemination of knowledge is not leading unequivocally to greater democracy. The advent of leisure—in the industrialised societies—has not brought personal fulfilment but greater mass manipulation. The economic and military unification of the world has not brought peace but genocide. The peasant suspicion of "progress," as it has finally been imposed by the global history of corporate capitalism and by the power of this history even over those seeking an alternative to it, is not altogether misplaced or groundless.

If one looks at the likely future course of world history, envisaging either the further extension and consolidation of corporate capitalism in all its brutalism, or a prolonged, uneven struggle waged against it, a struggle whose victory is not certain, the peasant experience of survival may well be better adapted to this long and harsh perspective than the continually reformed, disappointed, impatient progressive hope of an ultimate victory.

Finally there is the historic role of capitalism itself, a role unforeseen by Adam Smith or Marx: its historic role is to destroy history, to sever every link with the past and to orientate all effort and imagination to that which is about to occur. Capital can only exist as such if it continually reproduces itself; its present reality is dependent upon its future fulfilment. This is the metaphysic of capital: the word *credit,* instead of referring to a past achievement, refers only to a future expectation. Such a metaphysic has come to inform a world system and has been translated into the practice of consumerism. The same metaphysic has lent its logic to the categorization of all those who are being impoverished by the system as *backward* (i.e., as bearing the stigma and shame of the past). This trilogy has been written in a spirit of solidarity with the so-called "backward," whether they live in villages or have been forced to emigrate to a metropolis. Solidarity, because it is such women and men who have taught me the little I know.

PIG
EARTH

A Question of Place

OVER THE COW's brow the son places a black leather mask and ties
it to the horns. The leather has become black through usage. The
cow can see nothing. For the first time a sudden night has been
fitted to her eyes. It will be removed in less than a minute when
the cow is dead. During one year the leather mask provides, for
the walk of ten paces between fasting-stable and slaughter-house,
twenty hours of night.

The slaughter-house is run by an old man, his wife, who is
fifteen years younger, and their son, who is twenty-eight.

Seeing nothing, the cow is hesitant to move, but the son pulls
the rope round her horns and the mother follows holding the cow's
tail.

"If I had kept her," the peasant says to himself, "another two
months until she calved. We could not have milked her any more.
And after the birth she would have lost weight. Now is the best
moment."

At the door to the slaughter-house the cow hesitates again. Then
allows herself to be pulled in.

Inside, high up near the roof, is a rail network. Wheels run on
the rails and from each wheel a bar hangs down with a hook on
the end of it. Attached to this hook a horse's carcass of four
hundred kilos can be pushed or pulled by a fourteen-year-old.

The son places the springed bolt against the cow's head. A mask
at an execution renders the victim more passive, and protects the
executioner from the last look of the victim's eyes. Here the mask
ensures that the cow does not turn her head away from the bolt
which stuns her.

Her legs fold and her body collapses instantaneously. When a viaduct breaks, its masonry—seen from a distance—appears to fall slowly into the valley below. The same with the wall of a building, following an explosion. But the cow came down as fast as lightning. It was not cement which held her body together, but energy.

"Why didn't they slaughter her yesterday?" says the peasant to himself.

The son pushes a spring through the hole in the skull into the cow's brain. It goes in nearly twenty centimetres. He agitates it to be sure that all the animal's muscles will relax, and pulls it out. The mother holds the uppermost foreleg by the fetlock in her two hands. The son cuts by the throat and the blood floods out on to the floor. For a moment it takes the form of an enormous velvet skirt, whose tiny waist band is the lip of the wound. Then it flows on and resembles nothing.

Life is liquid. The Chinese were wrong to believe that the essential was breath. Perhaps the soul is breath. The cow's pink nostrils are still quivering. Her eye is staring unseeing, and her tongue is falling out of the side of her mouth.

When the tongue is cut out, it will be hung beside the head and the liver. All the heads, tongues and livers are hanging in a row together. The jaws gape open, tongueless, and each circular set of teeth is smeared with a little blood, as though the drama had begun with an animal, which was not carnivorous, eating flesh. Underneath the livers on the concrete floor are spots of bright vermilion blood, the colour of poppies when they first blossom, before they deepen and become crimson.

In protest against the double abandonment by blood and brain, the cow's body twists violently and its hind legs lunge into the air. It is surprising that a large animal dies as quickly as a small one.

The mother lets go of the foreleg—as if the pulse was now too weak to count—and it falls limply against the body. The son begins to cut the hide away around the horns. The son learnt his speed from his father, but now the old man's actions are slow. Ponderously at the back of the slaughter-house the father is splitting a horse in two.

Between mother and son there is a complicity. They time their work together without a word. Occasionally they glance at each other, without smiling but with comprehension. She fetches a four-wheeled trolley, like an elongated, very large open-work pram. He slits each hind leg with a single stroke of his tiny knife and inserts the hooks. She presses the button to start the electric hoist. The cow's carcass is lifted above them both and then lowered on its back into the pram. Together they push the pram forward.

They work like tailors. Beneath the hide, the skin is white. They open the hide from neck to tail so that it becomes an unbuttoned coat.

The peasant to whom the cow belongs comes over to the pram to point out why she had to be slaughtered; two of her teats were decomposing and she was almost impossible to milk. He picks up a teat in his hand. It is as warm as in the stable when he milked her. The mother and son listen to him, nod, but do not reply and do not stop working.

The son severs and twists off the four hooves and throws them into a wheelbarrow. The mother removes the udder. Then, through the cut hide, the son axes the breast bone. This is similar to the last axing of a tree before it falls, for from that moment onwards, the cow, no longer an animal, is transformed into meat, just as the tree is transformed into timber.

The father leaves his horse and shuffles across the abattoir to go outside and pee. This he does three or four times each morning. When he walks for some other purpose, he walks more briskly. Yet it is hard to say whether he shuffles now because of the pressure on his bladder, or to remind his much younger wife that, whilst his old age may be pathetic, his authority is remorseless.

Expressionless the wife watches him until he reaches the door. Then she turns solemnly back to the meat and starts to wash it down and then to dab it dry with a cloth. The carcass surrounds her but almost all tension has gone. She might be arranging a larder. Except that the fibres of meat are still quivering from the shock of the slaughter, exactly as the skin of a cow's neck does in summer to dislodge the flies.

The son splits the two sides of beef with perfect symmetry.

They are now sides of meat such as the hungry have dreamt of for hundreds of thousands of years. The mother pushes them along the rail system to the scales. They weigh together two hundred and fifty-seven kilograms.

The peasant checks the reading on the meter. He has agreed to nine francs a kilo. He gets nothing for the tongue, the liver, the hooves, the head, the offal. The parts which are sold to the urban poor, the rural poor receive no payment for. Nor does he get paid for the hide.

At home, in the stable, the place which the slaughtered cow occupied is empty. He puts one of the young heifers there. By next summer she will have come to remember it, so that each evening and morning, when she is fetched in from the fields for milking, she will know which place in the stable is hers.

Death of La Nan M.

When she could no longer
prepare mash for the chickens
or peel potatoes
for the soup
she lost her appetite
even for bread
and scarcely ate

He was painting himself
black on the branches
to watch the crows
who no longer flew high
but kept to the earth

Smaller than the stove
she sat by the window
where outside the leeks grow

By the wood stack
— the hillsides of brushwood
she had carried on her back—
he crouched and became
the chopping block

Her daughter-in-law
fed the chickens
put wood in the stove

At night he reclined on each side
of the black fire
burning her bed
What she asked him was his opposite?
Milk he answered with appetite

Lining the kitchen
family and neighbours followed
her fight for breath

High up the mountain
he pissed on
snow and ice
to melt the stream

She found it easier if
she laid her head
on the arm of the chair

His urine was the shape
of an icicle
and as colourless

In her hand
she held a handkerchief
to dab her mouth
when it needed wiping

On his black mirror
there was never breath

The guests as they left
kissed the crown of her head
and she knew them
by their voices

He trundled out a barrow
overturned it
on the frozen dungheap
its two legs still warm

The seventy-third anniversary
of her marriage night
she spent
huddled in the kitchen
from time to time calling her son
she called him by his surname
who rocked on his slippered feet
like a bear

One mistake you made
Death did not joke like a drunk
You should not have grown old

I was not a thief she replied

Dead she looked as tall
laid out on her bed
in dress and boots
as when a bride
but her right shoulder
was lower than the left
on account of all
she had carried

At her funeral
the village saw the soft snow
bury her
before the gravedigger

A Calf Remembered

HUBERT LED THE CALF into the lorry and unbuckled her collar. Later he would hang it on a nail in the hayloft, ready for the next calf. He was a large man, but very meticulous. The travelling buyer from the plant asked him his price. When Hubert did not wish to talk about something, he had the habit of making speech-like noises which in fact did not form words, but were convincing and sounded like another patois. If Marie asked him where he had been working, and his thoughts were still far away, he would answer in this polite unintelligible language. He did this now to force the buyer to name his price for the calf. The price did not, as it does for most livestock, go by weight but by look. Folding the bank notes, Hubert made a little square packet of them, and thrust it into the depths of his trouser pocket. Then both men went up to the kitchen to drink a glass of gnôle.

Whenever Hubert had passed the calf in the stable, she backed away abruptly and clumsily. She was attached close to the wall by a chain and a collar. The largest movement she could make was to lunge with her head at the bottom of the wall and kick her hind legs in the air. The lower part of the wall was brown from the shit of the other calves who had been attached to the same ring in the wall.

She did not have a name, because Marie did not give names to calves they were not going to keep. When the calf was ten days old, she had been timid. This was at the end of February. The streams from the rockface were as idle and transparent as icicles. The calf slept on the wood put down on the stone floor to keep her warm. She stood waiting to be fed. She learnt to kick. She came to recognise the pressure of the collar round her neck when she moved a certain distance away from the wall. She distinguished between near and far. An approach towards her from far to near became a threat.

When she was five days old, Hubert tied a child's plastic bucket round her muzzle to prevent her trying to eat the straw of her bedding. Only a little daylight entered the stable. Perhaps the half-light encourages the great winter patience of the cows. For six months they face the same beams, the same wooden struts of the same manger. Between their four stomachs, they fill their time with eating, munching, re-munching, licking, slowly lowering and raising their heads. They never—not even during the night—relapse into the non-being of the reptile or sleeping bat. If they did, they would produce no milk.

Some calves drink straight away, some have to learn. She would push with her nose against the side of the bucket without opening her mouth. She was two days old and her tongue had not found a way out of her mouth. Hubert stuck his finger into the milk and put it into her mouth. She sucked it. The third time he did it, her tongue came out to lick.

At dawn the cold intensifies. The apple trees had been black in the white mist. There was no colour anywhere, and beyond the yard no sounds. The north-east wind was blowing. It penetrates the thickest clothing and blows in one's very bones a reminder of death. It causes the cows to give less milk. It makes the earth hard as rock. "There is nothing sadder than a death," said Marie, "and nothing forgotten more quickly."

The wind could not penetrate the stable directly. The stable had the banked, three-month-old heat of one large horse, eleven cows, five calves and a dozen rabbits. But Hubert took no unnecessary risks: he tied a large piece of sackcloth over Moselle, the cow who had just calved, and gave her hot cider with sugar.

Before that, he had given her salt. Powerfully, with her enormous tongue, Moselle licked the coarse brown salt from his hand. Cows' heads are the size they are to contain their tongues. With their tongues they harvest, fork, bale and deliver to their stomachs.

There is a story about a distant ice-age and a cow who was called Audumla. She licked an iceberg in which a man was imprisoned. She licked it like a pillar of salt, until the man was free. And then she offered him four streams of milk.

The calf's first taste in life had been salt. Hubert rubbed some against her muzzle. Then he covered her with straw and she fell asleep.

Mucus is a protection, a kind of love. The calf lay there exhausted, like a leaf when it first comes out. Her hair was matted with mucus. Faintly she had the smell which once preceded—for all of us—the first smell of air. Hubert rubbed the calf down as if he were a second in a ring. His happiness was without excitement; it was a drawn-out pleasurable response to something occasional but familiar; a response to an event which gave itself to the stillness which now followed it, like the last note of a fanfare still hanging in silence, the trumpeter's arm still raised. His happiness took the form of a small drawn-out feeling of pride which lasted all day.

Before rubbing the calf down, he had separated its hind legs to discover its sex. Female. Perhaps some of the rabbits were bucks, otherwise all twenty animals in the stable were female.

Marie had turned Moselle's head round towards the tail, towards the birth. With one hand she held a horn and with the other she pressed with fingers and thumb in the animal's huge nostrils. "There Moselle," she repeated, "there Moselle!" Holding the head like this made it impossible for the cow to get up on to her feet. Moselle was lying on her left side. Two of the calf's hooves were already visible. Hubert made slip-knots at either end of his rope and passed them over the hooves on to the forelegs. Then, with his boots wedged against the gutter, he lay back on the rope and pulled. He saw the calf's head, an eye with its long lashes still closed, come out. He pulled harder on the rope until he was almost parallel with the floor. The vagina yawned, and the entire calf emerged like a sound, accompanied by two little rivulets of blood.

Hubert had called Marie half an hour before. Moselle had been kneeling on her forelegs, searching low down with her mouth and pointing her rump at the sky. She licked the air beyond her mouth, and her mouth itself was drawn back in pain. Her lower flanks shrank and expanded irregularly; waves of uncontrollable energy filled and emptied them; most of the waves broke in her chest before they reached the uterus. A calf's hoof, brown and white, smeared with a little blood as if it were being eaten, pointed out of her vagina and was sucked back in again.

It was dark. Hubert lay on a bale of straw which he had brought down in preparation for the birth. Muguet pissed. Marquise, next to her, waited and then pissed too. It went like that for four cows down the line. The cocks were not yet awake. Hubert got up to piss in the same gutter. He was anxious. The year before, when Moselle calved, she had a twisted uterus and he was obliged to call the vet which cost money.

On all four legs Moselle moved backwards, arching her back and raising her tail. She did not lift it straight up as she did when pissing; it was curled so that it made a kind of tail halo above the swollen distended vagina. The way she moved backwards was not as if she yet needed to push something out of her, but because, vaguely, she sought something behind in the dark air to push into herself, to rid her of discomfort. Hubert had not turned on the light because he believed calves were born quicker in the dark. Through the window at the end of the stable he could see the moonlight. The mist which would thicken at dawn was not yet thick enough to hide the moon. He felt his way into her with his hand. She spread as easily as a haversack. He felt the head between the two forelegs in the opening where it should be. This was the first time the calf had been touched.

Marie had stayed in bed. It was 2.00 a.m. Crossing the yard his boots had struck the ice as if it were metal. Perhaps somewhere in another valley a neighbour was also getting up for a calf. But in the colourless night there was no sign of it. A dribble of viscous uterine water hung from her vagina.

He sat on a milking stool in the dark. With his head in his hands, his breathing was indistinguishable from that of the cows. The stable itself was like the inside of an animal. Breath, water, cud were entering it; wind, piss, shit were leaving.

Often he dozed off. He thought of how each week now a little more light entered the hayloft above, as the great stacks of hay diminished and the sun shone a little brighter through the cracks in the planks. In three months' time he would let the cows out into the fields which would be green, sprinkled with white and blue flowers and dandelions. The cows can smell the green grass even in the stable. And their shit would become green. Sometimes he lurched, almost falling off his stool.

The unborn calf already had the capacity to see, and this developed capacity, along with others, predicted an end. The calf's capacity to see was waiting for the darkness to be broken.

Hubert had slept, his head fallen forward, his chin on his chest.

In the darkness, which precedes sight or place or name, man and calf waited.

Ladle

Pewter pock-marked
moon of the ladle
rising above the mountain
going down into the saucepan
serving generations
steaming
dredging what has grown from seed
in the garden
thickened with potato
outliving us all
on the wooden sky
of the kitchen wall

Serving mother
of the steaming pewter breast
veined by the salts
fed to her children
hungry as boars
with the evening earth
engrained around their nails
and bread the brother
serving mother

Ladle
pour the sky steaming
with the carrot sun

the stars of salt
and the grease of the pig earth
pour the sky steaming
ladle
pour soup for our days
pour sleep for the night
pour years for my children

The Great Whiteness

ALL THE DEAD are remembered at La Toussaint. Some say it is the day when the dead judge the living, and that the flowers placed in the cemetery are to make their judgement less harsh.

A week after La Toussaint Hélène came down to the cemetery to remove two pots of chrysanthemums, one from the grave of her husband and the other from her father's grave. For the last two nights the sky had been exceptionally clear, the stars as hard as nails, and the frost had nipped all the life out of the flowers. If she took them now, before the frost entered the roots, she could plant them out next spring, and in the late summer they would flower again to appease the dead.

At the foot of her husband's grave, she said, "Only two or three bones are left." Then she made the sign of the cross, not against her black coat, but over the ground into which he had been lowered.

At the foot of her father's grave, which had no masonry but only a wooden cross, she said: "Ah my father, if you could see your daughter now."

She did not hesitate to speak her thoughts out loud.

The cemetery, like everything else, was on a slope, and so she left by the top gate so that her climb home would be shorter. She carried a pot in each arm, the tousled blossoms, the tips of whose petals had gone brown with the frost, were level with her head on each side. She was a woman of seventy-five.

In the house she took off her black overcoat and put on an apron, a cardigan and a grey shawl over her head. "There's still time!" she said to one of her goats, leading it out of the stable.

The goat ambled lightly along the path beside her in the forest.

As Hélène walked her boots made a scuffing noise in the leaves, which in places were covered with frost like grey salt. She led the goat with a short rope, and in her other hand she carried a stick. After half an hour, she stopped under an oak tree and filled the large pocket of her apron with acorns.

"Jésus Marie!" she said to the goat. "Aren't you ashamed? An old woman collecting acorns for you."

The goat looked at her through the black oblong centres of its eyes. A few specks of snow, no larger than sawdust, fell between the trees.

"The great whiteness will soon cover us," she said and tugged the rope.

"Sometimes I try to pray, but things come into my head and distract me. It's my nature. My poor father told me the same thing. You're always wanting to be in the oven and the flour mill at the same time, he said, and so you can't keep your mind on anything. I'll tell you what you are like, he said, you are like the man whose friend says to him, 'I'll give you my horse if you can say the Lord's Prayer without thinking about anything else.' And the man says, 'Done.' And he begins, 'Our Father which art . . .' "

The old woman and the goat could hear the roar of the stream ahead. The stream was so full that its water frothed like milk.

". . . and when the man gets half-way through the Lord's Prayer he stops and says, 'Can you give me the bridle for the horse too?' "

Everything was grey except for the rushing water and the white flecks of snow on the goat's neck. The path left the forest and climbed between fields. The goat started walking faster, pulling the old woman along. She was the stronger of the two, but instead of checking the goat, she trotted behind. In one place the path was entirely covered with ice.

Cows place their feet with a certain delicacy as if wearing high-heeled shoes; goats, however, are like skaters. The goat danced on the ice and Hélène, letting go of the rope, gingerly felt her way round the edge, holding on to the grass bank. When she was on the other side of the ice, the goat refused to come towards her. She threatened and raised her stick. "It's snowing," she muttered, "it's nearly night. As if all my losses aren't enough, shit, shit, shit, you are playing me up."

On some occasions anger made her cunning. When she let out her chickens and they began to pull up the flowers in her garden, she pretended she had grain in her hand for feeding them, and she clucked sweetly to attract them, until she could lay her hands on one: then she would shake it with both hands and its feathers would fall out and she would hurl it above her head as high as she could against the sky. And the chickens were so stupid they came one by one to get their punishment.

The goat, who was not stupid, stared at her as she waved her stick. "You good-for-nothing carcass of a goat!"

After a while the goat stepped off the ice and the pair of them continued on their way. The very desolation of the scene made them look like accomplices. The rockface rose up above them, sheer as a wall for three hundred and fifty metres. The massive pine trees at the top were just visible in the falling dusk, as small as sprigs of herbs.

Hélène led the goat towards the wall, at the same time calling. Her call was not unlike the noise she made to attract the chickens when she fed them. But it was a shriller and shorter call, punctuated with silence.

After several calls there was an answering one which no voice could have imitated. Perhaps an instrument like a bagpipe would come nearest to reproducing it. The lament of breath issuing from a skin bag. The Greeks called the cry of the he-goat *tragos,* from which they derived the word tragedy.

He was darker than the surrounding dusk and his four horns were entwined with each other, as can sometimes happen with the branches of a tree when the trunk has divided into two. His gait was unhurried.

Hélène hid her left hand in her right armpit to keep it warm. With her right hand she held the rope. The goat stood there waiting. The specks of snow were turning into large flakes. Since she was a child she had done the same thing when the first real flakes fell. She stuck out her tongue. The first snowflake prickled like sherbet on her seventy-five-year-old tongue.

The goat lifted her tail and began to wag it. It made a circular movement like a spoon stirring quickly. The he-goat licked beneath it. Then he straightened his neck and the corners of his lips curled back baring his mouth to the taste. His thin, red-tipped penis emerged from its tuft of hair. He stood as motionless as a boulder. And after a moment his penis retracted. Perhaps the occasion was too inauspicious even for him.

"Jésus, Marie and Joseph!" muttered Hélène. "Hurry, will you! My hands are getting frozen. It's night."

He sniffed and let the goat's tail brush between his eyebrows.

If the snow fell all night, she would be unable to bring the goat again, and she would have one or two kids fewer to sell in the spring.

The he-goat stood there as if waiting for something to pass. In her impatience Hélène squatted down on her heels, the snow settling on her shawl, to look under his body to see whether all hope had gone. There was still a tip of red.

"If I turned my anger into power," she muttered, "it would blow up that wall of rock. Hurry! Will you?"

The he-goat tapped the flank of the goat with one of his forelegs. Several times. Then he tapped her with his other leg on the other side. When she was in position, he mounted and entered her.

Nothing else anywhere under the wall of rockface was visibly moving except the snowflakes and his haunches. His movements were as rapid as the falling flakes were slow. After thirty thrusts, his entire body shook. Then his forelegs slid off her back.

Hélène pressed with all her weight on the centre of the goat's back. This was to encourage the retention of the sperm. The pair set off down towards the village. They took a longer but wider path down, past the house where Arthaud lived.

Lloyse, Arthaud's wife, was killed by a boulder which fell from the top of the rockface. They were both asleep in their bed. Where the boulder first hit the earth, it made a hole big enough to bury a horse in. Nevertheless the boulder continued to roll down the slope. Slowly. When it reached the house, it didn't crash right through it. It just broke through one wall and crushed half the bed. Lloyse was killed outright and Arthaud woke up, unhurt, beside the boulder. This was twenty years ago. The boulder was too heavy to move. So, clearing the wood and rubble away, Arthaud built another room on the other side of the house and in this room he now slept.

When Hélène and the goat passed, there was a light in the window of this room and one side of the boulder was already glistening with snow.

Hélène placed her hand, whose joints were swollen so that she could never fully straighten her fingers, on the animal's back. "Goat," she said, "lazy good-for-nothing carcass of a goat, don't lose it!"

The spermatozoa who had survived the beginning of their long journey were swimming inwards in anti-clockwise spirals.

The wind was blowing the snow in whorls and she walked holding the goat's collar in case she slipped.

Easter

By night the icicles
grow longer
teeth of transparent rodents
by day they dribble
from food of snow

The white sheet removed
is folded in streams
my orchard
a morgue of branches
severed from the apple trees

Water furtively
unbolts the slopes
the prisoner grass is freed
pallid harrowed
too weak to make a sign

The cock's footprint
arrow of soil
brown as the dungheap
wide as the sky
is about to cover the hen of the world

An Independent Woman

CATHERINE SEIZED EACH MAN to embrace him. Her long arms pulled him towards her tall body. First Nicolas her brother, then Jean-François the neighbour. She kissed them on both cheeks, near the mouth. At seventy-four, she was just the eldest of the three.

"It's buried one metre deep," said Catherine, "I can hear Mathieu telling me that. One metre deep."

"Where does it cross the field?" shouted Nicolas.

She shrugged her shoulders. "Fifty years is a long time, but I remember him saying it was one metre deep."

Two months ago, when she was helping her brother bring in his second hay, she had told him that the water to the *bassin* beside her house was no longer flowing. After that, she had refused to mention the subject again. She was going to be dependent on nobody. Yet now the expression in her eyes was excited as though she had willed the two men to come.

"The spring must be at the top," said Jean-François and he began to climb the field, disappearing into the fog.

"Jean-François," she cried out, "come back before I lose sight of you."

Born into another house Catherine would surely have married, but each year of her life more men had left the valley, and she herself had inherited too little to propose to any of them that they remain.

She seized hold of Jean-François by the arm. "You shouldn't have come to give up a whole day."

"We dig one metre deep, at right angles to the line. Begin at the top and come down to the bottom. That way we're bound to arrive at the pipe."

"And the pipe will lead us to the spring! Jésus, Marie and Joseph! We'll have it by midday."

They began digging. Underneath the snow, the ground was still unfrozen.

When Catherine came from the house, carrying in a canvas bag glasses, a jug of hot wine and some bread and cheese, she heard the men before she could see them. At a distance of twenty metres the white fog merged into the white snow on the ground. Each time Jean-François bent his back to strike the pick into the earth, he grunted. And she heard Nicolas scraping his spade so the earth should not stick to it.

She had worked once as a waitress in a café near the Gare de Lyon in Paris. She and her brother Mathieu, the one who had laid the pipe and the one who was killed by the Germans during the Occupation, were the first members of the family ever to earn wages. And to do this they both went to Paris. He was a porter. She was a waitress. Her lasting impression of the capital was one of money continually changing hands. There, without money, you could literally do nothing. Not even drink water. With money you could do anything. He who could buy courage was brave, even if he was a coward.

The two men had dug the trench exactly one metre deep. From time to time they had measured it. It was straight and impeccably cut and cleaned out. On one side was stacked the turf; on the other, the earth. All the stones lifted out were piled in a heap together.

Nicolas scrambled out of the trench and Jean-François plunged his spade into the loose soil, as if in the hope that it would disappear into the centre of the earth. Living by himself in the corner under the mountain, he had the habit of making violent movements; in his solitude such violence was a kind of company. Catherine poured out the hot wine. The men kept the glasses up to their faces between sips, their noses in the steam which smelt of cloves and cinnamon.

"In God's name it must be here," Nicolas grumbled.

"I tell you if it's not in this field, there's no fire in hell."

During the second half of the day Nicolas continued the long trench already begun. Jean-François dug another higher up. And Catherine started digging a third near the pair of apple trees. When she had cut the turf, she kicked the snow off before lifting the pieces up. She disliked having cold hands or feet. At night she took three hot bricks to bed with her, one for each foot and one for the small of her back. As she swung the pick the breath came out of her with a whistle, quite unlike Jean-François' grunt.

After working in the restaurant by the Gare de Lyon she became a maid in a doctor's house. The doctor worked at the hospital of St Antonine and lived a few streets away in the rue Charles V. Her principal jobs were cleaning grates, washing floors and laundering. The first time she laundered, she had asked the cook where the wood ash was kept. "Wood ash!" repeated the cook, incredulous. "To clean the sheets," explained Catherine. The cook told her to go back to her goat shit. It was the first time Catherine heard the word *peasant* used as an insult.

They dug until the fog absorbed the dusk.

Jean-François looked down at his trench which was now a good fifteen metres long.

"Not quite wide enough for a coffin."

"We are all of us thin," said Catherine.

"Three graves, one for each of us."

"A grave for each of us!" roared Nicolas.

When she returned from Paris, Catherine had found her sister-in-law dying of puerperal fever. During the next fifteen years she brought up her two nieces like daughters.

Jean-François abruptly picked up a stone and threw it up the field into the dark.

Catherine began hustling the two men towards the house. Outside the kitchen door she placed a bowl of heated water for them to wash in. She took hold of Jean-François' wrists and placed his hands in the water. Then she draped a towel round his neck.

The last time the three of them had sat round the table in the kitchen was when she believed she might die. The doctor said it was pleurisy. She refused to go to hospital. If she was going to die, she wanted death to pass by the things she knew. Her two rooms were bare, there was neither armchair nor carpets nor curtains. But there were certain objects which were intimate to her: her yellow coffee-pot, the stove which she kept as shiny as a groomed black horse, her high bed, the picture of the Madonna above it, her work-basket. Death must run the gauntlet of these. Each night she laid out her linen and stockings before climbing into the bed, so that Nicolas should know exactly how to dress her for the coffin.

One night when he came to the house, Nicolas noticed the linen laid out.

"What's that for?"

"To dress me in the morning if I shut my umbrella in the night." She spoke in a hoarse whisper.

At that moment there was a scuffling noise against the door and a voice had intoned, like a lament:

"Four wild boar! I've seen them with my own eyes, charging down the hill!"

Jean-François had stumbled in, clutching a rifle. Drunk, he came up to the bed.

"Catherine, what will we do without you? They tell me you are very sick."

"Is the gun loaded?" she whispered.

He handed it to her and she took out the cartridges.

When she was working at the doctor's house, she had received the letter from Mathieu saying that his wife was ill and that she must return immediately. By leaving so abruptly she lost two months' wages. She protested to the doctor's wife that nobody could foresee illness. For illness there are hospitals, was the reply. Catherine picked up one of the pokers she had polished every morning. The doctor's wife screamed for help. The cook came running to the rescue. She found the mistress of the house clutching the curtains as if she had been surprised naked. And the mad Savoyard maid was standing with a poker in her hand looking at the fire.

"Tomorrow," Jean-François said, "we'll come and cup you. Eh, Nicolas?"

"I might be better off on the other side," she said.

"Seigneur!" screamed her brother. "Stop talking like that. We're coming tomorrow."

When they came, the two men stuffed the stove with wood. She stripped naked to the waist and sat on a chair. "It's not the first time you've seen a woman," she said to Jean-François.

"What difference does that make?" demanded Nicolas. "We're going to cure you."

On the table was a set of glasses with a candle. Jean-François lit the candle, wiped a glass, tore a shred of newspaper, put it in the candle flame and when it was burning, placed it in the glass. Nicolas pressed the rim of the glass hard against his sister's back. Almost immediately the flame went out. The skin beneath her shoulder-blade was white and soft, not very different from when she was a young woman. Tentatively, Nicolas' large hand abandoned the glass to see whether the vacuum would hold it against the flesh. Glass and flesh stayed firm.

Jean-François prepared the fire in a second glass.

"Put it," he said, "where there's plenty of meat."

"Never on the vertebral column," proclaimed Nicolas.

"I said where there's meat!"

They applied five glasses. Her skin rose up inside them like pies in an oven. She held the table with her arms to steady herself against the hurt.

"I don't want you to hear me cry out."

"I'll sing," offered Nicolas.

He sang:

> *La vie est une rose*
> *La rose piquera . . .*

When it came to removing the glasses, Jean-François did it because Nicolas' nails were too broken. He ran his finger-nail round the rim of the glass, making a tiny trench in the flesh, to let the air in.

"Ah," she sighed, as each glass came off. "Thank you, my friend!" Two days later she was cured.

Now together in the same kitchen the three of them were dispirited by the day's work which had yielded nothing.

"They have a machine," mused Jean-François, "for detecting water underground, like a water diviner's stick, only it's electronic. And it finds where water is to twenty centimetres."

"Where?" asked Catherine, on the edge of her chair.

"It costs seventy thousand francs to hire."

"Merde de merde!" said Catherine.

Next morning the three of them surveyed the three trenches. During the night, as if encouraged by their digging, moles had thrown up their own earthworks over most of the field. This made all the digging look less systematic.

"In this earth," roared Nicolas—and between each phrase he struck with his pick—"in this damned earth of this damned field in this damned fog I have a rendez-vous with the Devil!"

By the afternoon they had still not found any sign of any pipe. Occasionally in the kitchen Catherine heard one of their raised voices. She could not distinguish the words but the tone of the shouting was enough to tell her how discouraged they must be. "If they don't find it today, they won't come back tomorrow."

She put more wood on the stove, took her slippers out of the oven and shut the oven door. "I have wasted two of their days," she muttered. She set about preparing some pastry. When it was rolled out, she made small pastry purses, each large enough to hold a five-franc piece. Into the purses she put purée of apples. She made twenty-five.

She packed the pastries with the coffee-pot, *gnôle* and cups into her canvas bag, and strode across the orchard. Before the men became visible through the fog she stopped and adjusted the scarf tied round her head. She held out the bowl of sugar so that each man could sugar his coffee to his taste. She herself poured the eau-de-vie plentifully into their cups. The men held them with both hands and gazed around them into the fog.

"Mathieu!" muttered Nicolas. "Mathieu was cunning. He could have laid this pipe at a depth of eighty centimetres and it would still have been safe from the hardest frost. But no! Not Mathieu. He had to lay it at a metre!"

"The moles have eaten the pipe."

"The pipe has gone to La Roche, I tell you!"

Corner by corner, she unfolded the napkin wrapped round the pastries. Baked a light brown, they steamed in the air. The smell made the two men glance at each other and smile with complicity.

"We used to eat them after midnight mass at Christmas," said Nicolas quietly.

"The blood's coming back," said Jean-François.

Between mouthfuls of coffee, they ate them one by one.

When they were finished, Catherine issued her command: "No more work today."

The two men put on their coats and, by an accord of common tact, nobody mentioned tomorrow.

She woke up when it was still dark. She did not expect the men to return for a third day's work. After she had fed the goats and cleaned the stable, the sky was as blue and large as it only is over the mountains. In the valley, through the transparent early-morning mist were church, dairy, cemetery, two cafés, post office: the village. The worst about real fog is that it hangs square like a curtain. Vertical and horizontal. The best about it lifting is that all the slopes are revealed and everything is precipitous.

She went to fetch her water, downhill, across two fields. She had done this ever since the water had dried up. All her father's life and grandfather's life the sound of water had marked the place below where it was easy to fill buckets.

What she feared was the ice. The ice would soon be back. The pine trees, only one hundred metres higher up towards La Roche, were white with hoar-frost, not a needle, not a spider's web had escaped its white load. She feared that when the slope was frozen with ice, she might slip as she carried the buckets, and break a leg, and lie there all day without being found.

"On the other side I'd have no goats to look after, no potatoes to lift, no chickens to feed. I would have all the time in the world, and I could make all the visits I don't make now. Yet I don't want to die out of the house. I want to see death come past the things I've lived with. Then I can concentrate and not be distracted."

In the clear air which no longer muffled sounds, she heard Jean-François' voice, high up, in the field by the orchard.

"I tell you where it is! Here! Here is where I am betting it is! You'll see. I thought about it in the night. This is where it is. Within half a metre of here!"

Leaving the two buckets, she clambered up, shouting, "I don't believe it!"

They did not begin digging where Jean-François had driven in his spade to mark his bet. They systematically extended the long trench which would eventually come to the point he had indicated.

After two hours, Nicolas said: "The earth has been worked here. Fifty years ago maybe, but the earth has been worked here."

The only sign of his impatience was that he wielded the pick with shorter pauses.

"I told you so!"

He pointed, at the bottom of the trench, to a reddish mark in the earth, the size of a small flower.

"Rust!"

"Rust!"

"Catherine!"

The three of them looked down at the pipe at the bottom of the trench.

"It's in perfect condition."

"It's a well-turned pipe."

Jean-François jumped down and scratched at it with his knife.

"The metal is shiny underneath."

"I knew it when we saw the rust."

"It was there all the time," shouted Nicolas.

"The pipe under the field was there all the time."

"Exactly one metre down. Measure it."

Jean-François measured it.

"Exactly one metre."

"All we do now is to follow it."

"The spring should be here."

They stood looking down at the coarse grass.

"We'd have found it yesterday if we'd gone on," Nicolas shouted. He surveyed everything: the snow peaks, the rockfaces, the white forest, the ledges of land, the valley. "You'd have found it, Catherine, if you'd dug another two metres by the apple trees." He gazed up at the spaceless blue sky. "I'd have found it if I'd dug upwards instead of downwards! And Jean-François found it where he said he would!"

Impatiently Catherine started cutting the turf. The two men ambled away, opened their trousers and pissed.

They unearthed the reservoir after half an hour's further digging.

"It's a huge stone," announced Jean-François, "it must be two metres wide, the lid."

Nicolas peered at the flat stone being uncovered. "Where could he have found a stone like that. From La Roche!"

"We'll need crowbars to prise it off."

"Is it all one stone?"

"He placed it well, he knew how to place it, did Mathieu. I told you he was cunning."

"It's going to weigh a ton!"

"How did he get it here?"

"It's huge."

"As huge as a tomb."

"It's Jésus' tomb!"

"Jésus' tomb," repeated Catherine.

Jean-François scraped at the stone, his unshaven face almost touching it.

"We've got to roll it away."

Catherine went to fetch what bars she could find in the stable. They forced in two to steady it, and they used one to prise with. The flat stone did not shift. All three strained to use all their weight.

"Jésus'. . . tomb!"

"We're opening it."

"Op—en—ing!"

"Up!"

"Up!"

"What's inside?"

Jean-François peered through the narrow space under the prised-up flat stone.

"Shit!"

"He says Jésus' tomb is full of shit!"

"Fifty years of shit!" said Catherine.

"Slide it now."

"Gently."

"There!"

In the great current of their triple laughter, words they had already used surfaced, turned and eddied, disappeared, reappeared and were carried on, submerged by the laughter.

—Jésus, Marie and Joseph!—

—Mathieu knew what he was doing!—

—It was easy for him.—

—It's big enough to dip a sheep in.—

—The tomb of Jésus, that's what it is.—

They plunged in their arms up to their armpits, to find where the outlet pipe was. Their arms came out black. With a bucket they began emptying out the sediment, until the water no longer overspilled.

"Run to the *bassin,* Catherine, and see if it's coming."

"It's coming," she screamed. "It's coming out brown like coffee."

The sun had set before they stopped dredging.

The men carried the tools to the house. Close against the wall, in the shelter of the eaves, water gushed out of the mouth of the pipe. As it fell, it became tangled and silver.

Inside the kitchen it was warm. Catherine strode around the room, particularly between stove and table, serving.

"Sit down, woman!"

"I never expected you to come today," she said.

"Tonight it's going to freeze."

"The water from the spring will never freeze," she said.

"Today is the last day we could have dug."

"This morning I never said you'd both come."

"Catherine, you have always expected too little," Jean-François announced.

"Listen a moment!" roared Nicolas.

The three of them placed their knives on the table and through the window they listened to the frivolous sound of the running water.

Ladder

The uprights are pine
the rungs are ash
between each rung
the grass of months is pressed
hard as a saddle

At the foot of the ladder
on her back
belly distended
like a grey risen loaf
a dead ewe
legs in the air
thin as the legs
of a kitchen chair
she strayed yesterday
ate too much lucerne
which fermenting
burst her stomach
the first snow
falls on her grey wool
a vole in the dark
systematically
eats the ear on the ground
at daybreak two crows
haphazardly peck
the gums of the teeth
her frosted eyes are open

Every ladder
is lightheaded
on the topmost rung
the seeds have flowered
into the colours of the world
and two butterflies white
like the notes of an accordion
pursuing
touching
parting
climb the blue sky

Far above the ladder's head
instantaneously
their white wings change into blue
and they disappear
like the dead

Descending
and ascending
this ladder
I live

The Wind Howls Too

SOMETIMES WHEN I listen to the wind howling at night, I remember. There was very little money in the village. During eight months we worked on the land to produce the minimum of what we needed to feed and clothe and warm us for the whole year. But in the winter nature went dead, and it was then that our lack of money became critical. Not so much because we required money to buy things, but because there was so little to work with. This, and not the cold or the snow or the short days or the sitting round the wood stove, is why in winter we lived in a kind of limbo.

Many of the men went from the village to Paris to earn wages as stokers and porters and chimney-sweeps. Before the men left they made sure that there was enough hay and wood and potatoes to last until after Easter. Those who stayed behind were the women, the old and the young. During the winter the fact that I had no father was scarcely remarkable; half the children of my year were temporarily without fathers.

That winter my grandfather was making a bed for me, so that I shouldn't have to sleep any more with my sister who was soon to be married. My mother was making a mattress of *crin*. *Crin* was the hair of the mare's mane and cows' tails. Every morning, when it snowed in the night, my mother announced the news in the same way. "He has served us some more!" she said. She spoke about the snow as if it were uneatable food.

After the cows had been milked, my grandfather and I cleared the snow from the courtyard. This done, he went to his carpenter's bench and I, before going down to school, made sure that no snow was covering the stone sabot. If it was, I brushed it off.

The stone sabot was in the courtyard near the wall, beside the door to the vaulted cellar where the potatoes and turnips and a few pumpkins were kept. When we cleared the courtyard we did not always clear right to the edges, and so there was a risk that the stone sabot might disappear under the snow. Winter was the season of disappearances. The men went away. The cows were hidden in the stables. Snow covered the slopes, the gardens, the dung-heaps, the trees. And the roofs of the houses, covered by the same snow, became barely distinguishable from the slopes. Not since I first found the stone sabot had I let it disappear.

It looked like this. Its stone was whitish, marked with blue. It was a man's size. It was too large for me if I put my foot on it. The first time I saw it, I tried to pick it up to compare it with the pair of sabots, made from walnut wood, which were at the bottom of the wardrobe. The man who made the wardrobe took a winter making it and my great-grandfather paid him by cutting stones for his new house. The man's initials were *A.B.* and my great-grandfather carved these above the door to his house. I had seen them. When he was young, A.B. cracked many jokes. Later he was much given to thought, and finally he killed himself in the new house with his initials above the door. When I tried to pick up the sabot, I could not move it.

"Pépé, why is there a stone sabot in the courtyard?" I asked my grandfather. He was my authority about everything which was mysterious. It was several months before he answered my question.

One evening, he told me, his father, my great-grandfather, came through the door from the stable into the kitchen—the same kitchen in which we lived—and announced: "Néra has put my eye out." "Aiee!" screamed his wife, but when she looked at him she said, "No, your eye is not out." He had very blue eyes. "She butted me," he insisted, "as I was feeding her."

Pépé looked into his father's face. Miserably and terribly during the next five minutes one of his blue eyes turned entirely red, blood red, and he never saw out of it again. Nor did he ever recover from the shock of losing this eye. He believed himself repulsively disfigured.

Glass eyes were not easy to find. One day a friend drove by cart to A . . . and there in a barber's shop he found a whole bottle of them. "Give me the bluest you have," said the friend. Pépé's father would not wear it. Instead, Pépé, who was the youngest of three sons and his father's favourite, had to walk in front of him whenever he went out, to warn those they met not to look into his father's eyes.

One year later Pépé announced to the family that he was leaving. He was going to Paris. The family could not live off four cows. His brothers did not argue with him, for it was either him or one of them who had to go. He was fifteen at the time. His father ordered him to stay at home.

As he was packing his bundle, he found a pair of his father's boots. They were the newest and strongest boots in the house, and he put them on. His father was working in a circle of rocks above the house. He climbed the slope to embrace him. Then he pointed to the boots on his feet, and, as he was running down, he shouted: "The good ones are going! The bad ones are staying!"

In Paris he worked for several years without returning. The last job he had was on the building site of Le Grand Palais, which was to house the world exhibition to celebrate the opening of the century.

Whilst he was absent, his father, peering out of one eye, cut the stone cross and headstone for his own grave. On it he carved his name and added the date of his birth, 1840, the year that Napoleon's body was transferred from St Helena to the Invalides. Then he carved the supposed date of his death. The latter proved correct, for he died before the year was out. I passed the grave in the cemetery. And the date of Napoleon's home-coming I learnt at school.

When Pépé came back from Paris he found the stone sabot in the courtyard. He said his dead father had put it there as a sign that he had forgiven him for taking the boots.

That was all.

"How do you know your father forgave you?" I asked him after a long while.

"Nobody can take the stone sabot," he explained. "It's fixed to the rock. It'll outlast the house. And *that* is what is important. The boots I took were unimportant. He wanted me to know that."

The way Pépé told me this story made me think he had never told it to anybody else. His telling me was a privilege. I kept the stone sabot clear of snow because I recognised this. Whenever he saw me bent over the sabot, he smiled.

The Sundays passed. We became vague about the date. In limbo one loses a sense of time. My mother kept on repeating, "He has served us some more!" Repeatedly we cleared the courtyard. The pile of snow in the corner grew and became as high as a room. Every day two pairs of crows perched on top of the same apple trees. My grandmother hated them because they tried to eat the grain she gave her chickens. Pépé claimed that one of the crows was older than he: "I'd give a lot," he mumbled, "to see all that he has seen—the fights, the legal battles, the zouaves, the inventions, the couples in the forest . . ."

One evening in January my grandfather took the decision. "Tomorrow," he said, "we are going to kill the pig." On the day we killed the pig everybody had a job to do. And from that day onwards we knew that, however distant it still was, the spring was approaching. The mornings would get lighter. Not regularly, but when there were no clouds in the sky.

I went with my grandfather to look at the pig.

"He's as long as a pew," said Pépé with pride.

"He's bigger than last year's," I said, wanting to share in the pride.

"He's the biggest I remember. It's all those potatoes Mémé feeds him. She'd feed him her own dinner if she had to."

He ran his hand along the length of the pig's back, as if celebrating the virtues of my grandmother.

Mémé had found it difficult to make up her mind whether to marry Pépé or not. There was a photograph of the wedding in their bedroom. With the money he had saved whilst working in Paris, he had bought out his brothers, and the family farm became his. In the wedding photograph their two faces were unlined and round like apples. Even in the wedding photograph Pépé looked cunning. He had the eyes of a fox, watchful, canny, with a fire in their darkness. Perhaps it was the look in his eyes which made her hesitate.

Pépé confided to his friend Marius that Mémé couldn't make up her mind whether or not to marry him. After the story of the stone sabot, he told me many stories of his life. The two friends planned a practical joke. Exactly that. A joke that would prove useful.

On the Sunday before Easter, Pépé suggested to his sweetheart that they take a walk together through the forest. By that time the violets and white wood anemones are out. One day it may be warm enough to undress; the next it can snow. The afternoon of their walk it was cold. He led her to a disused chapel where, inside, they were protected from the wind. He kissed her and put his hand on her breast. "The chapel was not consecrated," he said to me gravely. She started to undo her blouse. He didn't say this to me. He said: "I began to caress her." I pictured the breasts to myself when he told me the story.

Suddenly they heard a key turn in the door and the bell above the roof began to ring a tocsin: the peal used to warn people against fire, or to keep lightning away in a storm. The couple were trapped there in the chapel. Pépé pretended to look for a way out. My grandmother adjusted her chemise, pushed him towards the door and clung to his back. She was convinced that they had been caught by robbers, and could scarcely hear what he said for the noise of the bell.

The neighbours came running through the forest and saw Marius astride the roof of the chapel ringing the bell like a madman. They shouted to him but he couldn't hear. All they could see was that he was either crying or laughing. When he climbed down he solemnly put his finger to his lips and opened the chapel door. When the couple came out, he said: "There are two things nobody can hide—a cough and love!" Next Sunday the banns for their marriage were announced.

Pépé began to talk with the pig in the stable. To each kind of animal Pépé spoke in a different voice, making different sounds. With the mare he spoke softly and evenly, and when he repeated himself, it was as if he was speaking to a companion who had become deaf. To the pig his language was full of abrupt, high-pitched sounds, interspersed with exhaling grunts. Pépé sounded like a turkey when he spoke to the pig.

"Ahir ola ahira Jésus!"

Whilst he made this noise, he fitted a noose round the pig's snout, being careful not to let it tighten. The pig followed him obediently, past the five cows and the mare, through the stable door and into the sudden harsh light of the snow. There the pig hesitated.

All his life the pig had complied. Mémé had fed him as if he were a member of the family. He, for his part, had put on his kilo per day. One hundred and forty kilos. One hundred and forty-one. One hundred and forty-two. Now, for the first time, he hesitated.

He saw four men standing before him, their hands, not in their pockets to protect them from the cold, but held out in front. He saw my grandmother waiting in the kitchen doorway without a bucket of food. Perhaps he saw my mother staring with anticipation through the kitchen window.

In any case, he put his head down and with his four small feet beneath their gigantic hams, he stepped one step back. Pépé pulled the rope and as the noose tightened, the pig screamed and tried to back away. For an instant Pépé held the pig by himself. Nothing could drag him against his will. The next instant the neighbours were there pulling on the rope too.

Pépé's friend Marius and I pushed from behind. Every feature of the pig, except his mouth, is small. His arsehole is no larger than a buttonhole in a shirt. I held him by his tail.

After five minutes of dragging and heaving, we had him across the yard, alongside the large wooden sledge. This was the sledge that killed my father.

Pépé and my grandmother had waited four years for a child. "The weather and the cunt," Pépé said, "do what they want." My father was their first-born. Two years later came my aunt. They had no other children. And so, as soon as he was old enough, Pépé needed my father to work. The sledge killed him when he was thirty and I was two. He was bringing down hay from the alpage. The path was steep and about three kilometres long. In places it was cut through the rock, in places it was muddy, in places it was paved with rough stones around sharp, heavily banked corners. We used this path to take the cows up to the alpage in June and bring them down at the end of September. When I helped Pépé drive them up, he never stopped at the place where his son was killed. There was an overhanging grey rock there, which bulged outwards like the side of a whale. Not on the way up, on the way down, in the autumn, we always stopped under this rock and Pépé said: "This is where your father lost the heart to go on."

We needed to get the pig up on to the sledge, lying on his right side. During the struggle across the yard, he had planted his feet as hard as he could against the ground in order to resist being pulled by the rope and being pushed from behind. When he felt himself being toppled, his four legs lunged and searched for the ground with desperate speed and force and at the same time he yelled louder. Never before had he discovered his strength as he was discovering it now.

The men threw themselves on him. For a moment he was invisible beneath the heap of men, and he lay still. I could see one of his eyes. The pig has intelligent eyes, and his fear was now intelligent. Suddenly, lunging and kicking, he fought like a man, a man fighting off robbers.

During the next twelve months he was going to give body to our soup, flavour our potatoes, stuff our cabbages, fill our sausages. His hams and rolled breast, salted and dried, were going to lie on the rack, suspended from the ceiling above Pépé and Mémé's bed.

Grunting and using our knees and fists we got him still. Pépé roped three of his feet to the side bars of the sledge. As soon as a foot was tied, the pig struggled with all his strength to tug it from the knot. I climbed up to sit on his haunches. The men were swearing and laughing. As Mémé crossed the courtyard, I waved to her.

The day my father was killed, he had already brought down three loads of hay. It was in November, just before the snow. The hay is piled high on the sledge and tied down. At the top of the path, before the descent, you get between the shafts, tug once, and then brake the sledge as its runners slide down over the stones and the leaves and the dust for three kilometres. You brake it by digging in your heels and leaning backwards against the load. If, at the top, you reckon the load is too heavy, you tie logs to the back of the sledge and let these trail on the path, to act as an additional brake.

Nobody knows what happened when my father brought down his fourth load. He was found dead under the sledge. People said he ought to have been able to push the sledge off his chest. Perhaps that November afternoon, before the winter, his exhaustion or sadness was so great that he could not summon the will. Or perhaps the sledge stunned him.

My grandmother shouted at me: "You be careful he doesn't kick you!" Then she gave Pépé the knife, a small one, no longer than the ones used at table, and she knelt on the ground with her basin.

Low down, Pépé made a very short cut, from which the blood gushed out, as if it had always been waiting to do just that. The pig struggled knowing it was too late. The five of us were too heavy for him. His screams became deep breaths. His death was like a basin emptying.

The other basin was filling up. My grandmother, squatting on her haunches, was stirring and agitating his blood, to prevent it curdling. Every so often she took out and threw away the white fibres forming in it.

His eyes were shut. The space in him, left by the blood, was being filled by a kind of sleep, for he was not yet dead. Above the sledge Marius was gently pumping the left foreleg up and down so as to empty the heart. Pépé looked at me. I thought I knew what he was thinking: one day when I am too old, you will kill the pig!

We fetched the pétrin. It was long enough for a man to lie down in. Before we rolled him into it, we arranged a chain like a belt for him, so that when he was wet we could still turn him round by pulling on his belt. To fill the pétrin like a bath took two milk churns of hot water. He lay there almost entirely covered. Scraping his skin with the sides of tablespoons we shaved him, and the more closely we shaved him, the more his skin looked like that of a man. In the hot water his hair came off easily. He did not look like a man from the village, for he was too fat and too untanned, but like a man of leisure. The most difficult parts to shave were his knees, where the skin was calloused.

"He prayed more than a monk," said Marius. "Day and night he prayed to his trough."

When he was perfectly naked, with even the cuticles removed from his toes, Pépé put a hook through his snout and we hauled on the pulley to hoist him up. The pulley was attached to a wooden balcony where I often played as a small child. The only way onto the balcony was through a door from the hayloft; there were no stairs, so my mother knew that when I was there, playing and crawling on all fours above the courtyard, I was out of harm's way. The pig was larger than any of us. The men threw buckets of water over him, and to celebrate, they drank their first glass of *gnôle*.

Once Pépé spoke to me about death. "Last night," he said, "I was dragging some wood down with the mare, when I felt death was behind me. So I turned round. There was the path we'd come down, there was the walnut tree, there were the juniper bushes, there were the boulders with moss on them, a few clouds in the sky, the waterfall in the corner. Death was hiding behind one of them. He hid as soon as I turned round."

The pig's hind legs were ten centimetres off the ground.

"Head from body in ONE!" Pépé shouted and severed the head in one long cut with his small knife.

The body fell.

"The head for you!" he nodded towards me. I knew what I had to do. I took it, and ran up the pile of snow in the courtyard so fast that my feet made footholds and I reached the top. And there on the white summit I placed the pig's head.

The men were drinking their second glass of gnôle.

Into each hind leg, between the two bones, Pépé inserted a small hook. This time we hoisted up the carcass, neck down. The crows were too frightened by the men in the courtyard to approach the head on the pile of snow.

Delicately, from anus to neck, down the centre of the stomach, making an insertion with his knife, Pépé folded back the skin and fat. "Andre!" He said my name between his teeth because he was concentrating so hard.

He had made visible all that makes a pig a living, growing animal. All except the brain and head which were on the snow pile. The arrangement of the warm, steaming organs was the same as inside a rabbit. It was their size which was so impressive. When his belly was opened, it was like the mouth of a cave.

Pépé once admitted to me that he had dug for gold. During one summer he and a friend had got up two hours earlier every morning to go and dig there. They found nothing; but he showed me the shaft, should I ever wish to continue working it. It was hidden in a moraine on a steep wooded slope, where the boulders, the tree roots and the soil itself were all covered with a thick green moss. Whatever you touched there was like the fur of an animal.

I held one side of the zinc pan and Marius held the other, waiting for the guts and stomach to tumble out. Using only the point of his knife, as a woman does when unpicking stitches with the tip of her scissors, Pépé detached them. The grey guts overflowed the pan and we had to hold them in with our hands. They were warm and from them came the smell of killing.

The pig's liver, the pig's lungs, whitish-pink like two sprays of pear blossom, the pig's heart, Pépé removed separately.

I ran to the top of the snow pile again and turned the head round so that it faced its empty carcass. Underneath the head the blood had thawed a little snow, making a red cave. Standing on top of the snow pile, my head was level with the balustrade of the wooden balcony, where I had played when I could first walk. The men down below were throwing buckets of water over the carcass and rubbing it down, inside and out, with a cloth. Then they went in to eat.

Down the centre of the table were loaves of fresh bread and large bottles of cider. There were two kinds of cider, the sweet cider which we had pressed only two months before, and last year's, which was stronger. The older one was easy to distinguish because it was cloudier. Most of the women drank the new cider.

From a large black cast-iron pot on the stove, my mother filled the soup tureen to put on the table. To celebrate the killing of the new pig, we were going to eat what remained of the old.

In the soup, made with parts of the salted backbone, were carrots, parsnips, leeks, turnips. The loaves were passed round and held against each chest in turn, as a slice was cut off. Then, spoons in hand, we entered the meal.

Some of the men started to talk about the war. The body of another German soldier had been discovered a few weeks before in a crevice high up in the forest. This was the winter of 1950.

"If he'd stayed at home, he'd be sleeping today with his wife in his bed."

I was drinking the strong cider and listening to each conversation.

Every year, when the pig was killed, all the neighbours and Monsieur le Curé and the schoolmaster were invited to eat. The schoolmaster was sitting near Pépé at the head of the table. I was anxious in case he told Pépé about the hedgehog. The hedgehog was discovered in the schoolroom cupboard where the schoolmaster kept his coat. We called *him* The Hedgehog because his hair stood up at the back. He had very small hands too. And he wore glasses. Standing before the class, he invited whoever had put the hedgehog in the cupboard to remove it. Nobody got up. Nobody dared look at me. Then he asked: "Who knows why hedgehogs smell?" Like a fool, I put up my hand and said they made a smell when they were frightened.

"Then since you know more about him than any of the others, please remove him." The others began to laugh and some shouted Bravo! in such a way that he realised he had picked the culprit. As a punishment, he made me learn and recite out loud a page about hedgehogs. He brought the book himself next day, and I had to sit in the schoolroom until I had learnt it. I still remember how it began: "The fox knows many little things and the hedgehog knows one big thing." I wondered whether he had read the text himself, because a few lines further down it explained that, because of their spines, hedgehogs could not mate like other animals, but had to do so standing up, and face to face like men and women.

I was reassured, for the schoolmaster was making Pépé laugh. Opposite me La Fine, who lived below our fields and could take away the pain of burns, was telling a story about Joseph, her brother-in-law. He went to C . . . on a day when there was a fête and a band. He came back late at night convinced that in one of the cafés he had pissed into a golden lavatory! It turned out he had pissed into a bandsman's bassoon!

My mother never sat down. She went round the table serving. When she brought the stuffed cabbages on, we all cheered. "Wait till you taste them!" she cried, full of confidence. They had been cooking since early morning in a net in a deep pot. First she put a plate into the bottom of the net, then on the plate a layer of cabbage leaves, then a layer of stuffing of minced pork and eggs and shallots and marjoram, then a layer of leaves, then a layer of stuffing, until the net was as full and heavy as a goose. When I was younger I had watched her do it. Now I was drinking last year's cider like a man.

"I would like to know what life was like ten thousand years ago," Pépé was saying. "I think of it often. Nature would have been the same. The same trees, the same earth, the same clouds, the same snow falling in the same way on the grass and thawing in the spring. People exaggerate the changes in nature so as to make nature seem lighter." He was talking to a neighbour's son who was on leave from the army. "Nature resists change. If something changes, nature waits to see whether the change can continue, and, if it can't, it crushes it with all its weight! Ten thousand years ago the trout in the stream would have been exactly the same as today."

"The pigs wouldn't have been!"

"That's why I would like to go back! To see how the things we know today were first learnt. Take a chevreton. It's simple. Milk the goat, heat the milk, separate it and press the curds. Well, we saw it all being done before we could walk. But how did they once discover that the best way of separating the milk was to take a kid's stomach, blow it up like a balloon, dry it, soak it in acid, powder it and drop a few grains of this powder into the heated milk? I would like to know how the women discovered that!"

At the other end of the table the guests were listening to Mémé who was telling a story. There were two cousins in a nearby village who lived side by side because they inherited the same property . . .

"That is what I would like to know if I was a crow on a tree watching!" Pépé was saying. "All the mistakes which had to be made! And step by step, slowly, the progress!"

The two cousins fall out and start a fight. One of them bites a piece out of the other's nose. Both are too frightened to continue fighting. A few days later the bitten one is digging in his garden, with a cloth over his nose. He sees his cousin coming out of the house on the other side of the fence. "Well, well!" he shouts. "Are you feeling hungry today? Why not come over and finish off the rest of the nose?"

Whenever a plate was empty, my mother piled more stuffed cabbage on to it.

"The thread of knowledge which nature doesn't crush, like a thread of gold in the rock," Pépé was saying.

The faces shone in the heat, and the table became more and more untidy. My mother brought on an apple tart the size of a small cart-wheel.

"And then I would like to go several thousand years into the future."

"There'll be no more peasants."

"Not so sure! I didn't say forty thousand, I said several thousand! I'd look down at them like the old crow looks at us!"

Unless I concentrated on stopping them revolving, the walls of the kitchen would not stay still. On the table with the apple tart were cups of coffee and bottles of gnôle. I gulped down some coffee.

"All farms will be on flat plains," pronounced the schoolmaster.

The cold air of the courtyard cleared my head. At the end of the meal the guests left, saying, "Till the next time."

I wanted an excuse not to go down to school. The chances were not good, for the only possible excuse was that I was needed for work, and there was not enough work for me to do. I held the pig's forelegs whilst Pépé sawed the carcass into two from the back.

He put his shoulder under one of the sides, I unhooked it, he adjusted its weight, and he carried it across the courtyard, past the stone sabot, and up the outside wooden stairway to the room above the vaulted cellar. The side of the pig was longer than he was tall. He walked slowly, and on the stairway he stopped once. When he carried the second side, he stopped three times.

The next day he would cut the meat and lay it out neatly, like a flowerbed of pink delphiniums, on the trestle table. Every year he arranged it like this.

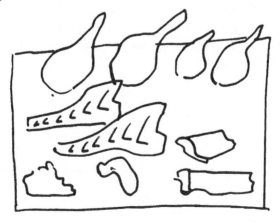

Then my mother would salt the meat in the wooden *saloir* and in six weeks Pépé and I would go looking for juniper branches for smoking the hams and the bacon.

The kitchen had been restored to its working tidiness. On the scrubbed table the women were cleaning the pig's guts and preparing to make boudin from his blood. Reluctantly I went down the steep path to school.

When I came out I had to screw up my eyes against the falling snow. Mémé did not warn me about bringing snow on my boots into the kitchen, because she was crying. She and my mother had laid Pépé on his bed.

He had collapsed in the courtyard. Tomorrow the same neighbours who had eaten lunch with us would be returning to pay their last respects to him.

No mountain in the world was as still and as cold as his face. I waited for his face to move. I told myself I would wait all night. But its stillness outdid me.

I went out and crossed the courtyard to look at the stone sabot. There was enough moonlight for me to see it.

I heard Pépé saying again: "That is what I'd like to know if I was a crow on a tree watching . . ."

During the night more snow fell, and in the morning, on top of the pile in the courtyard, I saw an unexpected shape, draped in white. I had forgotten the pig's head. Once more I ran full tilt up the side to the top. I brushed off the snow. The eyes were shut and the skin was as cold as ice. It was then that I started to howl. I do not know for how long I sat there, on top of the snow pile, howling.

Village Maternity

The mother puts
      the newborn day
           to her breast

turnips
      like skulls
           are heaped
                house high

before the blood has been washed
           from the legs of the sky

Addressed to Survivors

ROUSA BELONGED TO the breed which is called Abondance, after one of three sister rivers which flow through deep gorges with many waterfalls to the lake. She was reddish-brown and white, the white patches mostly occurring on the inside of her legs, her underside and her dewlap, so that she gave the impression of being a reddish-brown cow who had just waded across a river of milk. She had had four calves. Four times a perfectly formed animal with reddish-brown and white fur, the stumps of horns, hooves, eyelashes, teeth, ears, sexual organs, had grown in the matrix between her wide haunches and been expelled. Four times the birth had released a flow of milk into her immense udder which was like a full moon coming up behind a hill.

Martine owned six cows, and of the six, Rousa gave the best milk. After she had calved she gave as much as twenty litres a day.

"Cows are like distilleries," said Martine. "To have good milk, you need good pastures."

Her chalet in the alpage was high up the mountain. And the butter she made there was considered to be the best in the village.

Martine was in her mid-fifties. Her husband worked in one of the saw-mills of the valley. In the alpage her companion was an old man whom everybody called Joseph, although his real name was Jean-Louis.

Joseph had no family and came from another part of the mountains. He claimed to have been a shepherd all his life, which was probably true, but nobody gave great credence to his claims because he usually made them when he was drinking. He lodged with Martine and her husband, and in exchange for his keep he worked for them. If somebody in conversation asked: which Joseph? he was always identified as Joseph, The Servant of Martine.

"Rousa has turned mad," Joseph announced to her one evening.

"Why do you say that?"

"She's had three inseminations and not one has taken."

"We'll try a fourth time."

"She'll be on heat twice a month and turn mad. You should have sold her before," he muttered. "I said it when we were below."

"She is the best cow we have."

Martine had a light, lilting voice.

"I've been looking after cows for fifty years," he grumbled, "fifty years."

"You have no more wine, I think."

She said this, getting up from the table. She did not allow him access to the few litres of wine she kept for herself or for the occasional visitor. And he, for his part, never laid in a large stock. He preferred to go down to the village on the occasion of taking down their cheeses or fetching some bread, and to come back with four or five bottles in his haversack.

He ignored the remark about his wine.

"Women!" he continued. "When I was alone in the mountains, I kept the jobs to be done on one side, and the finished jobs on the other, and it was simple. When a woman is around, nothing is simple."

"Poor Joseph!"

"And now Rousa has turned mad!"

The chalet had one small dark wooden room like a sailing ship's cabin. At the end furthest from the door was a wooden platform which served as a bed.

He shuffled to the door without a further word. His moods could change very rapidly. When he was happy he pretended to dance through the door. When he was despondent he left the room as if leaving the world to its own damnation.

The room ran parallel to the stable and was only separated from it by wooden planks. From her bed Martine could hear a goat piss. But if the wall had been a hundred times thicker, she would have heard the blow that woke her that night. It reverberated as if the whole chalet had been struck.

They both got to the stable at the same time.

"What happened?" Martine asked.

The old man had excited eyes and looked cheerful again.

Rousa was on her feet staring at the torch light. The other five cows were lying peacefully on the wooden floor. The goats stared with their usual contradictory expression of surprise and mockery.

"It wasn't thunder," said Joseph. "The sky is . . ."

"What sort of noise was it?" interrupted Martine. "Did you hear it?"

"Yes I heard it."

"Were you asleep?"

"No."

"Then what sort of noise was it?"

"A noise like somebody trying to break through the floorboards. I thought it was you. I couldn't hear your voice. Something's happened to the Patronne, I said to myself. She needs me. I'm going down to her."

"See what you can see outside."

He walked out briskly, no longer shuffling, a man with a purpose.

"It's as calm as a lake," he announced when he came back. He had the habit of using turns of phrase quite inappropriate to the place or occasion, as if referring to something in his own past.

"It's a mystery," she said.

"I can tell you it was Rousa."

"I was dreaming of Rousa when the crash woke me up," said Martine.

The old man stepped closer. His brows, his temples, the bridge of his nose were wrinkled like the skin of baked milk. For a moment she hesitated, as if she were going to ask him something. Then apparently she decided against it. His past remained a secret not because he refused to answer questions—he always answered—but because the questions were bound to be wrong.

"Yes, I was dreaming. We weren't in the chalet here, we were down below. I'd gone to bed in the kitchen. This was in my dream. But earlier I'd asked you to help me push the bed, it was the big bed in our bedroom, the bed in which the Patron was born, to push it at an angle to the window. We pushed it together. This was to stop Rousa jumping out. The placing of the bed was a kind of barrier. Yet when I woke up I knew that Rousa had gone."

"Most dreams are foolish," he said.

Next morning, whilst he was taking the cows up to graze, she examined the stable to see if she could find any sign of what had woken them in the night.

Joseph's complaint that women always complicate work was unjustified. After ten summers in the alpage, the two of them did not have to discuss what needed to be done each day. He went out with the cows and goats; he brought them in; he cleaned the stable; he cut the wood; he looked after the horse. He treated the horse as if it belonged to him and not to the Patron. Perhaps this was by virtue of age, for the horse was thirty and he was seventy-six. "By the time of horses," he said, "he is older than me." Martine milked, churned the butter, made the cheeses, cooked for them both.

Now she examined the walls of the stable, the doors at either end, the wooden gully down which he shovelled the cow shit through a hole in the wall, the beams which were so low that he had to bend his head and she could just walk under, the manger and the chains for fastening the cows, and she found no clue to what it was that had woken them.

She went up to the loft. Nothing had fallen. The hole in the hay where he slept was deep. His few clothes were hung over a beam. As she was about to leave, she noticed the broken neck of a wine bottle just within reach of the hay. She knelt down to look for the rest of the bottle but found nothing. On her knees she could see between the floorboards.

She returned to the stable, lifted up her skirt and stood astride the wooden gutter into which the cows piss. Whilst relieving herself, she looked up. The floorboards over Rousa's place were gashed and one was completely split.

When he came back, she showed him the gashes in the wood.

"That's just below where I sleep," he said, "I tell you she has turned mad."

"How could she butt if she was chained?"

"When a cow turns mad, you'd be surprised what she can do. She can leave her skin and go right back into it again."

"Perhaps the gashes in the wood were there before."

"They could have been."

"Then what made the noise?"

"Rousa!" He screwed up his whole face because she would not see what was clear.

A few days later the cow tried to mount him.

"I saw her coming from behind. I was lucky enough to turn round and see her coming. She was charging down the hill and her forelegs were leaving the ground! She could have broken my back, five hundred kilos landing on it like that. Seventy-six years my back has kept me on these legs and they are not bad legs."

"What did you do?" Martine asked.

"They are the legs of a man."

"So what did you do?"

"I ran to the side and lay down."

"Lay down?"

"On the ground. So as not to give her a target. Not even a cow, turned mad, can mount a shadow on the ground."

She slapped her lap in amusement. They were sitting at the table finishing their soup.

"You are as thin as a shadow anyway."

His shoulders were large, but the rest of his body always looked hidden within the folds of his clothes.

"I knew I was safer on the ground."

"She might have trampled on you."

"If she'd mounted me, she'd have broken my back."

"God forbid!"

"I'm old, I'm nearer the big hole than the little hole through which I came into the world."

"But the little one still interests you!"

"Tomorrow I'll go down," he said, admitting no complicity and drinking the water out of his glass, "tomorrow afternoon."

"You can take the cheeses," she said.

He was quite content to sit in the darkness, smoking a cigarette and occasionally going to the door to spit. But the darkness irritated her unless she was in bed. If she was sitting up, she wanted to read. The books she liked best were about other parts of the world: China, Paris, Tahiti. Joseph's face was now barely discernible in the darkness. The lines and pouches on the faces of the other old people in the village could be allotted to events and experiences which were dated and recountable in detail; his remained mysterious, unrelated to any story, like the lines on the bark of a tree.

"I was thinking," he said, "she may have smelt me where I was sleeping above her."

Martine nodded. In the silent stable the cows were lying down. Outside, the mountains were reeling under the stars. That night Joseph went out of the room with one of his dance steps.

She took off most of her clothes. The two of them shared one broken piece of mirror, the size of a playing-card, which hung on the wall outside the door. In the mornings she did her hair in front of it, and once a week he shaved before it. Nobody in the alpage knows what they look like. She was standing in her bare feet when he came back.

"I tell you she has turned mad," he said.

"Never mind, Joseph, if you're right, we'll sell her in the autumn."

She climbed on to the wooden platform and bent double because of the low ceiling. From where he was standing he saw her white shape, vague but full like a cumulus cloud, trailing white legs.

"I'm not going to sleep in the same corner," he said, "it provokes her."

"You must do what you think."

"It might be best for me to sleep outside. She can smell me."

"Come, Joseph, you're not a bull."

"An old one, a very old one."

She laughed lightly from the depth of the wooden room.

Before he went down the following afternoon, he mumbled to her that she should keep an eye on the cows. Perhaps one of the reasons why the old are so rarely obeyed is that they insist so little on the truth of their observations, and this is because they see all such particular truths as small, compared to the immense single truth about which they can never talk.

When he returned with three loaves and five bottles of wine his eyes had a wide tearful look. This meant that he had drunk a bottle during the two-hour climb up. He went to fetch the cows and staggered once or twice against the slope, as if falling into the open arms of a new friend. Yet when he came back with only five cows, a quarter of an hour later, he was quite sober.

"Rousa has gone," he announced gravely.

"She must have wandered higher up."

"I went to look, there's no sign of her and I couldn't hear her."

"You don't hear well," she said. "I'll go."

"You can be deaf," he replied, "or you can be very sharp of hearing, but if there's nothing to hear, it doesn't make any difference."

"She has never gone off before."

"She never turned mad before. Yesterday she tried to mount me. And did I tell you what I did? I saw her coming and I lay down. Today she smelt a bull in the wind."

After the other cows were milked, the two of them set out to look for Rousa. The grasshoppers, with their back legs raised, kept hissing like snakes. It was possible to see for twenty, thirty kilometres. She strode faster than Joseph did, perhaps because she was more surprised by what had happened. The bells of the herds lower down sounded exactly the same as every evening. Yet Rousa was not to be found.

In winter it is impossible to remember exactly what cowbells sound like. One forgets, for instance, how at night they sound like stars clinking. In the same way it is impossible to recall, when once they have passed, how long the evenings are in June, when both light and mountains look equally permanent. In this horizontal endless light, towards ten o'clock, Joseph found Rousa lying in the grass, a hundred metres from the chalet. The sight of her, so reposeful and so near, startled him.

"Jésus!" he whispered. "How long have you been here?"

For an hour or so around midday the cows lay down to ruminate. When they got up that afternoon Rousa had strayed away from the others and climbed to the crest above the chalet. In her straying away there was already an unknown aim. From the crest she made her way down the other side, where rhododendra grow and where, in places, the slope is as steep as thirty degrees. A cow from the plains would have killed herself. But Rousa had spent six summers on the mountain. She even knew how to open the stable door if there was nobody there; she opened the door and the other cows followed her in. Rousa crossed the forest at the bottom of the next valley, picking her way carefully, because the creviced rocks and the roots of the spruces are like natural traps into which a heavy animal can fall and break a leg. Having crossed the forest, she climbed another crest so that she overlooked a third valley.

In this valley was a herd of eighty cows and two bulls. The bulls were white and belonged to the race of Charolais. Rousa mooed. She did not have to do this more than twice before one of the bulls recognised that the cow on the skyline was on heat. He climbed earnestly towards her. The second bull followed.

Did Rousa try to pull away from the great second white bull? Was she facing down the slope instead of up? Did her madness double so that she awaited a third bull or the return of the first? After receiving the first bull, was her appetite a little assuaged so that her back was able to bear less weight? The bulls weigh nearly a thousand kilos each. The questions will never be answered. The two bulls wandered down to join their herd and Rousa started her journey home.

When she was in sight of the door which she could open, fatigue overcame her and she lay down. Perhaps at this moment of her triumph, she was still unharmed. After resting, she knelt on her forelegs in order to get to her feet and reach the stable. But instead of being able to raise her hindquarters, those quarters whose insistent demand had forced her across a mountain, they toppled downwards, and her whole body followed. She was rolling down the slope. Each time her bent legs followed the arc of the sky and struck the ground again, she tried to dig them into the earth, and each time the momentum of her massive body was too much for her and she rolled another turn and with each turn she gained speed.

Joseph paced it out and found she had rolled a hundred metres. How she finally stopped herself was another mystery. He shrugged his shoulders. Yet she had stopped just in time. A few metres below, the slope increased to nearly forty-five degrees, and then nothing could have saved her. She would have hit the boulders at the bottom, a mass of unsellable broken meat and bone.

"Rousa's come back!" he shouted.

Martine came running, and stopped short to see the cow unexpectedly on the ground.

"Has she broken a leg?"

Joseph shook his head.

Together they pushed and pulled to get the cow on to her feet. She would not budge.

"We can't move her, the two of us by ourselves."

"In the morning I'll go down to get help," he said.

"I'm not leaving her alone all night," Martine insisted.

"A cow is an animal," he said.

"I'm staying with her. She could roll down there on to the rocks."

He walked away with his despondent walk.

"Twenty-seven years, and this is the first time I've had an accident with a cow." She said this quietly as she felt the cow's horns and ears. "A stupid accident. A stupid cow accident!"

With her complacent eyes Rousa followed the woman's movements. Her horns were unhealthily cold.

Joseph came back with some blankets draped over his shoulders. Something had mollified him.

"I will stay with her," he said.

"I won't sleep anyway," said Martine.

They spread the blankets over Rousa, and then over themselves.

"She knows what's happening," said Martine.

Cows rarely make any sound when in pain. At the most they blow heavily through their immense nostrils.

From under the blankets the two of them looked down at the far lights in the valley. The sky was clear, the Milky Way like a vast misty white goose pecking at the lip of a jug.

"If only she'd move," whispered Martine, "I could milk her."

She lay by the cow's head, the halter rope coiled round her wrist. He lay between the cow's four legs.

"The lights stay on all night in the villages," he said. "One, two, three, four, five, six, seven, but none of them is my village."

From out of his pocket he took a mouth-organ. He had had this mouth-organ for fifty years, since he was a conscript in the army. At that time, when he was young, he used to pretend to play an invisible trumpet, using only his lips and hands. If asked, he would entertain the whole barrack room by playing this trumpet which did not exist. One evening a friendly sergeant said: "You play well enough to have something to play on. Here, I've got two. Take this." And so he acquired a mouth-organ.

As he played now, he tapped his foot on the mountainside and looked at the tiny clusters of lights below—no larger than grains of sugar, fallen from a spoon.

He played a polka, a quadrille, a waltz, "The Nightingale of the Sweet Wood," a rigadoon. Neither she nor he could have said afterwards for how long he played. The night turned colder. As his foot beat time on the mountainside, his hands in the moonlight smoothed and ruffled each tune as if it were a bird miraculously perched on the instrument. All music is about survival, addressed to survivors. Once Rousa stirred, but she could not move her numb hindquarters.

When he stopped playing, Martine spoke very gently as if talking about a child being born. "I remember you used to play your mouth-organ when you first came to us."

"Twelve years ago."

"The Patron asked you"—she was laughing now—"if you could play The Charming Rosalie!"

"Twelve years and two months."

"You remember the month!"

"Yes it was April. There was snow. I knocked on the door and asked if I could sleep in the barn. You said Yes. The next day it thawed, and the day after I helped plant the potatoes. If it hadn't thawed that day, I wouldn't be here now."

"We had only daughters," she said, by way of explanation.

The two of them listened to Rousa's difficult breathing.

"The Patron is as cunning as a fox, isn't he? He used to leave money on the table. Did you know that? He used to leave it there at night to see if I was honest. One day I said to him, 'You needn't worry! I eat my own money but I'm not going to eat yours or the Patronne's!' "

The thought of this riposte of ten years ago made him burst into song:

> "Bon Soir! Bon Soir.
> You gave me the moon!"

When he could remember no more words, he continued on the mouth-organ. He serenaded her. He addressed her across Rousa's head, which rested on the ground. Every so often, out of tact, he looked away from her and across to the peak opposite. He played to the mountain and the woman. To the dead and the unborn.

Then, laughing, he broke into words again:

> "Bon Soir! Bon Soir.
> You give me the moon . . ."

On the last note his voice creaked like a pine tree in a storm. On the slope there was not a breath of wind. Then he pulled his beret over his ear and laid his head down to sleep.

Five minutes later Martine said: "If we can get her on to her feet in the stable tomorrow she has a chance. She wants to get up, I can feel it, Joseph."

He was already asleep with his knees drawn up. His open hand, palm uppermost, had fallen across the cow's udder. Beside it was an empty winebottle which he must have brought with him under the blankets.

Next morning eight neighbours came to pull Rousa, with ropes attached to each of her legs, across the grass and into the stable. They talked of using a pulley and rope to hoist her to her legs, but the stable ceiling was too low. After they had gone, Martine continued to puzzle on how she could save the cow.

She pushed planks under her in the hope of levering her up. She asked Joseph to stand on the far end of a plank. He jumped up and down with all his weight until he had to stop to pull up his trousers. But nothing moved the cow. The complacency of her look was turning into indifference. Her white patches were muddied with shit and with the soil she had been pulled across.

Between carrying out Martine's instructions, Joseph kept shaking his head.

Now she had the idea that they should nail blocks of wood to the floor by her hind feet, so that if she tried to get up by herself, she would have something to push against. Joseph cut the blocks of wood and nailed them to the floor.

The day the butcher's lorry came, Rousa was dragged through the door and up the ramp into the lorry. She made no sound. All she did was to roll her eyes, rolling them upwards, until only the blue-grey of the underneath of her eyeballs was visible.

In the lorry she tried for the last time to shift the dead weight of the body, muscles, tissue, organs, passages and vessels which had turned her mad for a bull, and had made her a cow with a yield of twenty-five litres of milk. But she couldn't. The cold from the mountainside was creeping up her back.

Martine stepped into the lorry and stuffed an armful of straw between Rousa's flank and the sharp metal housing round the back wheel. The road down was full of pot-holes, and she did not want the animal, who could not move, to suffer by her skin being chafed against the metal.

"She's a cow," one of the men said, when the back doors of the lorry were shut.

"A poor beast," said another.

Joseph stared after the lorry and remained standing in the middle of the rutted road long after it was out of sight.

"Hey, Joseph," a neighbour shouted.

He turned round, waved and made three dance steps.

"Come and have a drink!"

He disappeared into the stable where he looked at the horse who was older than him.

Sunset

Like a trout
our mountain basks
in the setting sun

as the light drains
the trout dies
its mouth open

the night
with its wings of spruce
flies the mountain

to the dead

The Value of Money

HIS FACE WAS THIN and his body was stocky. Sixty-three years old, his hair was still black. When he rode Gui-Gui, his work horse, there was a distinct resemblance between them: both were compact, like a loosely clenched fist. He sat high up by her collar, and he sat there firmly, as she, with her thick short legs, breasted the steep slopes.

He was the only man in the village who planted new apple trees. After the cider was pressed, he took an armful of *marc* and carefully buried it in the corner of his garden. The following year there were several shoots. He separated them out and mulched them, and in three years' time they were large and sturdy enough to plant out in the orchard. Later he grafted on to them.

The other men reasoned that the old trees—some of them were perhaps two hundred years old—would last their lifetime and that afterwards the orchards would be abandoned.

When I've gone, nobody is going to work my farm, one of them said.

We'll be in the orchard of the Dead! another shouted loudly, the very loudness affirming that they were not in that orchard yet.

Marcel, however, was a philosopher. In the evening he tried to explain to himself what had happened during the day, and thereafter to act according to his explanations.

This is how he explained planting the new apple trees.

My sons won't work on the farm. They want to have free weekends and holidays and fixed hours. They like to have money in their pockets so as to be able to spend it. They have gone to earn money, and are mad about it. Michel has gone to work in a factory.

Edouard has gone into commerce. (He used the term commerce because he did not wish to be harsh towards his youngest son.) I believe they are mistaken. Selling things all day, or working forty-five hours a week in a factory is no life for a man—jobs like that lead to ignorance. It is unlikely that they will ever work this farm. The farm will end with Nicole and me. Why work with such effort and care for something which is doomed? And to that I reply: Working is a way of preserving the knowledge my sons are losing. I dig the holes, wait for the tender moon and plant out these saplings to give an example to my sons if they are interested, and, if not, to show my father and his father that the knowledge they handed down has not yet been abandoned. Without that knowledge, I am nothing.

Nobody ever expected to see Marcel in prison. Often when a man's destiny suddenly changes as the result of his own actions, it is difficult to know how far back the story really began. I will only go back as far as the previous spring.

He was carting the winter's manure to the fields, distributing it in small piles about two metres apart. Later he would fork these piles evenly over the grass and earth. He carted the manure in a tipcart drawn by Gui-Gui. The similarity of build between horse and man had its usefulness. When the cart was full with a load of four hundred kilos, the young mare started hauling it up the slope as fast as she could, so as to gain momentum for the climb. Marcel, holding the bridle by her head, strode with her, and her forelegs and his legs kept perfect time. Fast time. Frequently they were forced to stop and regain their breath, before starting up again. Whilst they worked together, he talked to her, using a language of very abbreviated sounds to save his breath. These sounds had once derived from curt instructions or oaths; now they had left their meaning behind, and were just an accompaniment to the movement of their climbing legs. Sometimes he made these sounds in his cell in the prison at B. . . .

From the poultry house Nicole saw an unfamiliar tractor coming down the road. She waited to see where it would turn off. In the middle of the road, where no wheels went, the spring grass was already beginning to grow. At the side, on the banks, were clumps of violets.

Jésus! What is Marcel going to say? asked Nicole, as the tractor approached the farm.

She waved at her son Edouard on the driving seat. He drove past what remained of the manure heap and turned into the yard. There he climbed down and left the engine running. The tractor was blue.

I got it cheap, he shouted to his mother. It's twelve years old!

Nicole smiled encouragingly. She forgot anxieties as soon as they were over, and was reluctant to foresee the ones approaching.

He'll only be against it because he can't drive! Edouard said.

The father led the mare and empty cart into the yard. When he saw the tractor he stopped, and folded his arms on his chest.

What is it? he asked as if he had never seen a tractor before.

I've bought it! shouted Edouard against the noise of the engine.

The son stood with his elbow resting on the vibrating bonnet as if it were the shoulder of a girl, and his foot on the small front wheel. He was dressed in the clothes he wore to go to market: a pink shirt, blue jeans and ex-army suede boots.

The father would not approach nearer, and at such a distance the noise of the engine made everything inaudible.

What have you bought it for?

Nineteen sixty-three! bawled Edouard. Twelve years old.

It's only four months ago that I bought the new mare. Marcel seemed unaware that nobody could hear his words. When the horse butcher took the last Gui-Gui away, I came into the kitchen and I held up the empty bridle, the bridle she had worked with for fifteen years and I said to you: Do you know what this means? And you replied: It means a tractor! And I said: No, it means Gui-Gui has gone! It does not mean a tractor in God's name!

It'll pull twenty tons!

The motor hesitated and stopped.

What do you say? demanded Edouard.

I say it's no use to us! said Marcel, unharnessing Gui-Gui the Second, and leading her into the stable.

In the evenings Marcel became sleepy. The lids came down over his slate-coloured eyes and his lower lip protruded a little. It was then that he looked his age.

You were ungrateful, Nicole told him. He bought it out of his savings.

He bought it because he can't help buying, Marcel replied, yawning.

She nudged him, not angrily but brusquely, and handed him a brochure. He gave me this, to show you.

He turned the pages carefully as if turning them was the last job of the day. The backs of his hands were smooth, they might have been the hands of a baker; their palms were calloused and engrained like the wood of the tipcart.

They are beautiful, how could they not be beautiful? he said. Men have dreamt of machines like this for centuries. Who would believe that my mother carted earth in a wheel-barrow from the bottom to the top of her field for ten days on end? With a tractor it would have taken half an afternoon.

If we had that machine, we'd get the hay in in eight days!

LIBERATOR
avec encore plus de confort

They promise everything. Look at their colours—yellow, blue, red, bright green: they promise the world!

He walked to the door. False promises! He shouted the two words out very loud.

A few minutes later he came back, buttoning his fly.

Do you know what those machines are for?

They plough, they turn hay, they spread dung, they milk—it depends, answered Nicole.

There's one job they all do.

He looked into her eyes with the utmost seriousness. For all their experience, Nicole's eyes were innocent. They had seen illness, they had seen farms on fire, they had seen people work themselves to the grave, they had seen women agonising in labour, but they had never seen men poring over a map and drawing up a plan.

Their job is to wipe us out.

All Edouard did was to save enough money to buy a secondhand tractor, said Nicole.

Marcel took off his beret and his leather jacket and started unbuttoning his shirt. She looked straight at him.

You can't always expect things to stay the same, Marcel.

There are only two machines worth having here—

Nicole interrupted him.

Do you know what I think?

She was taking the pins out of her hair. Unpinned, it came down to her waist.

I think you're furious about the tractor because you can't drive!

If I wanted to, I could learn! Marcel answered.

This made her laugh. The flesh of her arms, immense after forty years of milking, moved as if she were dancing when she laughed.

Why not? he demanded.

Oh la! la! she sighed between bursts of laughter. What did I pick out of the lottery?

In the prison at B . . . , Marcel answered her question: she married a bandit without knowing it.

The day after Edouard bought the tractor, Marcel continued distributing the winter manure. The leaf-buds on the apple trees were opening, the tiny leaves so young that they were almost colourless, and wrinkled from being folded, like all new-born skin. His body felt old and its joints were stiff from the winter. Each forkload of dung had to be lifted into the cart. After filling three carts and stepping out each time with the mare as she tugged the cart to the top field, a hundred and fifty metres higher than the house, his spine pained him, and with every forkload lifted, two bars of ache twisted inwards at the bottom of his stomach making his balls hurt. That day the noises he made to Gui-Gui were sometimes the complaints of his own body.

The day before he had taken up twelve cartloads. His right elbow was sore and bleeding a little from where the striding beside the mare had knocked his arm against a harness hook on the horse's collar. One cart made four heaps, three dragged out with a hoe and the last one tipped.

He stood, looking down at the farm, the valley, the village, the cemetery, the road that led away. Whilst he stood there he didn't move any part of his body, so that all parts should rest. He knew exactly where he would lie in the cemetery. Looking down from there at the cemetery, he explained the machines to himself.

On the flat plains the poor have no choice but to work for the rich. By themselves the poor, working only for money, would have neither the energy nor the heart to produce enough to create wealth. This is where machines came in, long ago. Machines make monkey-work productive, and the wealth they create goes to those who own the machines. On the plains I would not have this hernia of an ache because a machine would be lifting dung onto another machine which would transport it and scatter it.

When he was reloading the cart in the yard he stopped to straighten his back. He could see the piles of dung arranged in three straight lines with geometrically regular intervals in the top field by the forest. At that distance they looked scarcely larger than the beads of a rosary. Seventy-two Hail Marys.

On the plains there will be no more peasants.

By the evening he had shifted his thirteen cartloads.

They had four children. Michel, their eldest son, and their two daughters, Marie-Rose and Danièle, were married. Edouard, who still lived at home, was the youngest. When he left the local school, Edouard had gone to the technical school at A . . . and there obtained his trade certificate as a garage mechanic. No jobs existing in the local garages, he went into a factory. After a few months at the factory he made friends with some forains and left the factory to begin working with them in the local markets. From an early age Edouard had the reputation of being lazy. He himself said: I'm willing to work as hard as the next person, but I'm not a fool and I'm not going to work for nothing.

Perhaps the attraction of the forains for Edouard was the pride they took in never being taken for fools.

First he sold biscuits and boiled sweets, later mirrors and painted trays. Once he brought home a tray for his mother. It had a stag painted on it. His father was enthusiastic. Look at him, he mused, in the forest! It's too good to use as a tray!

The tractor was a different matter. His father refused to acknowledge its existence. Two months passed.

One day in June, when the whole family came to help with the haymaking, the four grown-up children agreed amongst themselves to ignore the old man's opposition.

He's boneheaded! said Danièle. If we've got a tractor, why not use it?

When Marcel's back was turned, they tethered the mare in the shade of an apple tree, unbolted the shafts, and attached the blue tractor to the hay wagon. Everyone was waiting for the old man to protest and order them to put the horse back. They were going to refuse. To their surprise, Marcel said nothing. As usual he took his place on top of the wagon to build the load. At first he stood, and finally, when the load was three or more metres high, he knelt. Around the cart on the slope the women were raking. The men forked the hay up to him. He directed each fork where to place the hay, he folded the swaths in upon themselves, he constructed the corners and he keyed the corners into the centre. He built like a celestial mattress-maker, apparently oblivious or indifferent as to how the wagon would be drawn across the earth.

In the loft the heat and smell of the new hay was already like the breath of an animal. Marcel climbed one of the ladders to fetch a fork which had been left on top. The last hay had not yet lain down. Stalks of it waved slowly in the dim light under the roof timbers. Some of the wall planks had holes in them where their knots had once been. Through these holes came beams of sunlight, narrow as branches. When a stalk crossed a beam, it caught the light for an instant and lit up like a spark.

On top of the hay, he again explained the machines to himself. They make sure we know the machines exist. From then onwards working without one is harder. Not having the machine makes the father look old-fashioned to the son, makes the husband look mean to his wife, makes one neighbour look poor to the next. After he has lived a while with not having the machines, they offer him a loan to buy a tractor. A good cow gives 2,500 litres of milk a year. Ten cows give 25,000 litres a year. The price he receives for all that milk during the whole year is the price of a tractor. This is why he needs a loan. When he has bought the tractor, they say: Now to use the tractor fully you need the machines to go with it, we can lend you the money to buy the machines, and you can pay us back month by month. Without these machines, you are not making proper use of your tractor! And so he buys a machine, and then another, and he falls deeper and deeper into debt. Eventually he is forced to sell out. Which is what they planned in Paris (he pronounced the name of the capital with contempt and recognition—in that order) from the very beginning! Everywhere in the world men go hungry, yet a peasant who works without a tractor is unworthy of his country's agriculture!

In July the heifer Marquise mounted on Marcel's back, as if he were a cow and she the bull. Marquise was not yet fully grown. Her teats were no larger than the fingers of a woman's glove. Marcel fell forward onto his knees. For a week his left leg hurt and, after putting it off several times, he decided to go and see the bone-setter in A. . . .

It was market day and the bus was crowded. Marcel calculated that it was eight years since he had taken the bus. After half an hour, he could no longer name a single farm or hamlet which they passed.

The bone-setter grasped the old man's knee in his cool hands. The very white leg had no fat on it at all. The bone-setter rotated the knee and applied some ointment. Marcel paid the fee of three thousand francs and added a pot of honey. The bone-setter protested at the honey.

The honey is from our own bees, said Marcel.

The bus back was not until the afternoon, and so he wandered through the market. The tomatoes on the stalls were more advanced than Nicole's. Leaving the fruit and vegetables behind, he strolled between hanging carpets which were for sale. The sight of them and their thick pile made him thirsty. In a café he drank two glasses of cold white wine. When he came out, he saw a circle of people, mostly women, looking at somebody he couldn't see. The ones at the back were standing on tiptoe. From the centre of the circle he heard a man's voice, like a voice on the radio when the volume is turned up. Idly Marcel looked from woman to woman to decide which one pleased him most. She had wide hips and was wearing a dress with flowers like peonies printed on it, and was holding the hand of a small child. The voice of the invisible speaker continued:

Ladies, do I look like a crook? Did I hear one of you say Yes! Ah well! I know women are suspicious. And if I had to deal with men, like you do, I'd be suspicious!

Suddenly Marcel recognised the voice. The man in the centre of the circle was his own son. Cautiously he approached. He wanted to see without being seen. Edouard was wearing an apron over a bare torso. His shoulders and back were brown from the haymaking. In front of him stood a small folding table with some bottles and tins on it. He picked up a bottle and poured what looked like red ink from it, down the front of his white apron. The stain it made was the shape of a rabbit hanging by its hind legs, except that one front paw was longer than the other. Marcel's legs were trembling. His son took another bottle and poured a green liquid from it which ran down the overall like a stream and crossed the rabbit. The voice never stopped.

If you have children they spill things over themselves, if you have a husband—no, Madame, I'm not married—he starts looking into the engine of his car without changing his shirt, when you are going out for the evening, he tells you to hurry and you get nervous, you spill nail varnish over your new dress . . .

With two fingers, Edouard, his son, smeared silver varnish horizontally across the red rabbit on the apron over his stomach. Marcel regretted drinking the white wine because now, in the crowd and heat, he could not stop his legs trembling.

I take a brush, water and ordinary soap . . .

Edouard scrubbed down his stomach. His face was glistening with sweat, and when he paused between words, he kept his mouth open in a smile.

Soap, as you see, won't remove these stains . . .

At the ends of his long brown arms his fingers were coloured red, green, silver. Women in the front row were goggling at his shoulders, not at the monkey-work on his apron.

Now I'm going to rub with this unique cleaning tablet which removes grease, ink, coffee, wine, gravy—which removes everything except dried oil paint, and nothing can remove dried oil paint, it's like sin . . .

Marcel's mother, Edouard's grandmother, used to say, when she was in the yard at the washing trough: Water washes out everything except sin.

I take my cleaning tablet and gently rub. Up and down . . .

Jésus! said Marcel loudly.

Edouard spread his arms upwards like a Christ, and the apron, hanging from his neck, was white.

I'm not asking twenty francs. I'm not even asking fifteen. I'd be giving it away at ten. But because of that beautiful young lady wearing the dress with peonies on it, yes, Madame, you've melted my heart, I'M OFFERING IT TO YOU AT ONLY EIGHT FRANCS A TABLET. TWO FOR FIFTEEN. THREE FOR TWENTY!

It was not until several days later that Marcel confronted his son.

I saw you in A . . . the other day, said the father.

I heard you were there.

You were selling soap.

I've packed that in now. It was only a stop-gap.

Both men were standing in the kitchen, Marcel at the end where the floor was plain boards, Edouard by the sink where there was linoleum. Both of them were looking at the floor. Marcel raised his head.

You were robbing people. It was an authoritative accusation.

It took out a lot of stains, Edouard smiled.

Monkey-work! Why don't you practise your trade?

I like the outdoor life, I guess. He paused and then he shouted at the top of his voice, I must have got that from you! You wouldn't last a day in a factory!

The father shifted his legs, placing them wide apart, as if expecting to be jumped upon.

What you were doing in the market was fraud!

No, it was selling.

It was fraud!

It was selling!

In October Marcel and Nicole lifted the last potatoes. By November the small apples on the trees had turned red. Marcel climbed up to shake them down whilst the cows were still grazing in the orchard. Nicole waited in the cropped grass and the apples fell onto the sheet she had spread out. Each evening Marcel took the mare and tipcart and brought another ten sacks of apples up to the house. Altogether there were sixty sacks: fifty filled with apples and ten with pears.

As the afternoons became shorter, Marcel pressed the cider. The whole yard smelt of apples. He crossed it many times carrying buckets of apple juice to pour into the barrels in the cellar, and sacks of *marc* on his shoulder to empty into the vat. The vat was as tall as he and a good metre and a half in diameter.

One day, when the snow was not far away, Edouard came into the outhouse where the press was. Marcel scooped up a glass of apple juice and held it out to Edouard, who shook his head.

It gives me diarrhoea.

You can undo the press.

Edouard took off his belted raincoat and hung it on a nail.

You know, you could sell this thing as an antique, said Edouard, a wooden press with 1802 carved on it!

It's oak.

There's a dealer in A . . . who'd give half a million for it.

What would *he* do with it?

He'd sell it to a bank or hotel.

What?

As décor.

The world has left the earth behind it, said the father.

And what was on the earth? demanded the son angrily. Half the men here had to emigrate because there wasn't enough to eat! Half the children died before they grew up! Why don't you admit it?

Life has always been a struggle. Do you think it can ever be anything else?

You were dirt poor!

Marcel removed the fastening bolt without saying a word and the sides of the press opened. They were ribbed like a corset. Edouard lifted out the cake of *marc* which was as large as a cart-wheel, propped it on a bench by the window, and started to cut the *marc* into pieces with an axe. It was the consistency of damp bran and it smelt of all that had happened in the orchard since the spring.

It would be quicker to put it through the grinder, Edouard said.

It would be quicker but less good.

Why not use the grinder since you have it? Edouard insisted.

It makes better *gnôle* if you break it up by hand.

Why?

Marcel shrugged his shoulders. It's the nature of *gnôle*. I don't know why.

Edouard slashed violently with the axe at what remained of the wheel.

My father's a maniac, he hissed, a maniac!

When the vat was full Marcel covered the *marc*. The first layer of the covering was newspaper. The paper which came regularly each week into the house was the local one, full of reports of local councils, mayors' speeches, deaths, market prices, weddings and declarations from the Ministry of Agriculture. Over these news items he spread walnut leaves. And over the leaves he put earth. As the *marc* fermented each day and reduced its volume, he carefully pressed the covering a little further down.

The vat gave him pleasure, like the hay in the hayloft, or the smoked sausages, made from the pig, which hung from the ceiling above his high double bed. They were achievements which made him feel, as the snow obliterated everything on the ground, that the farm was prepared for the winter. The winter came.

Every pine needle was covered with hoar-frost. The fox stood there, surprised, as though at this season he did not expect to have to hide.

In God's name he can see I haven't brought my gun! whispered Marcel.

He had no means to kill the fox and the fox knew it. It was the same fox who had come down and taken nine of Nicole's chickens before the haymaking, when the grass was high enough to offer him cover. Now he was thin, his coat more grey than brown. Neither man nor animal moved. Faintly from a distant farm, both of them heard a cock crow.

What makes him shake his head like that? Jésus and Marie! He's cunning, cunning, more cunning than all the rest put together!

The fox, certain of his rights, walked unhurriedly up the slope between the juniper bushes and disappeared under the rocks and pine trees.

There I stood, explained Marcel, empty-handed, and I said to myself: Tomorrow I'll take the marc. It was the fox who made me decide.

He broke the seal and the initial smell of the marc gave off a kind of warmth in the cold air. He shovelled it into sacks and arranged the sacks in the tipcart. On the way down to the village he rode on the sacks. When he reached the cemetery he got down because there the road climbs.

It began to snow and he swore. As he looked up towards the sky he could see in the distance two electric light bulbs, strung from the tin roof of the engine. They were alight. When he arrived, Mathieu, the distiller, was wiping the sweat off his face despite the cold. Under the engine was a steaming heap of muck, the colour of bile, and every minute the snow falling on the heap made the muck less yellow.

How is the Patronne? Mathieu asked Marcel. She who was the most beautiful bride of her year, the most beautiful mother and now the most beautiful grandmother! The distiller bowed from the waist.

When Mathieu toured with the distilling engines he was expansive and gallant. The pace of the work and the cheating of the state out of some of its taxes inspired him. The rest of the year, working in a furniture factory, he was taciturn and hesitant.

Beechwood, good beef, and a beautiful wife—keep them whoever can! said Marcel.

His voice was gruff in the cold, and the snowflakes on his eyebrows were unmelted. He was still smiling with pride when he shook hands with the five or six men waiting by the engine.

The engine consists of a boiler, three vases and a condenser, mounted on an old chassis. The vases are insulated with planks of wood. The copper pipes which conduct the steam from the boiler to the vases and from these to the condenser are the thickness of a bull's horns. And they curve like horns too. At the bottom of the condenser was the outlet pipe and under it a small copper pail, filling up with *gnôle*. That the produce of this gigantic, shaking, copper-horned bull should come, drop by drop, out of a duct no larger than the open beak of a small bird, is a sign of its secret. Its secret is to transform work into spirit. What is emptied into the vases is work; what comes out of the beak is imagination.

Mathieu pulled a tragic face, waved his arms and bawled:

Shut off!

One of his assistants shut off the boiler, and the other climbed up to loosen the holding nuts which clamped the lids to the vases. Scalding steam hissed out from under the loosened lids and immediately turned as thick and white as smoke. From the tin roof a tarpaulin hung down to the ground to protect the waiting men from the weather. Between the engine and this tarpaulin, the white steam now made it impossible for the men to see their own arms.

They've come! said one of them, invisibly.

Who in God's name?

The steam turned wet on their faces.

The inspectors!

In the white cloud they all laughed at this joke for the inspectors had made their inspection only two days before.

When the steam dispersed they saw Mathieu holding up, with the handle of his hammer, a string of glistening black sausages.

Hand me a plate! he shouted.

Emile, who was born in 1897, stepped forward with a plate, and untied the tape which held the fur flaps of his cap over his ears, preparatory to eating.

Sausages, the colour of black cherries, cooked in *gnôle*, warm the heart because they are hot, arouse because they are salty, comfort because they taste of wood smoke, confer strength because they are meat, and release dreams because they are saturated with alcohol. Sheltered between the tarpaulin and engine the men ate. As they ate, the collars of their coats touching their cheeks, and the juice running out of the corners of their mouths, they grunted with pleasure.

Amen! said Emile.

Half-way through the morning, it was Marcel's turn to empty his sacks of marc into the vases. He had twelve sacks, enough to fill the three vases twice. Once more the bull engine started its work of transformation.

He had already filled three demijohns with gnôle when an old woman flung open a window in the nearest house and began to yell and wave her arms.

It's Marie, muttered Emile, she never lets me stay.

Reluctantly Emile left the engine and walked with his stick across the snow to his house. No sooner had he entered than he was out again waving his stick.

The men by the engine waved back at him, laughing, and continued to listen to the sounds of the copper bull. Soon they would say *Amen* again.

Mathieu! Mathieu! shouted Emile. Only when he had reached the engine did anybody take any notice of what the old man was trying to say.

The inspectors are coming! he gasped.

How do you know?

The baker telephoned. He said they drove past half an hour ago. The line was not working. Only just got through.

Everybody turned to Marcel.

How many litres have I got, a hundred? he asked.

I'm afraid so! said Mathieu.

Afraid so! My trees have never given so much as this year. Three thousand litres of cider! It's the best year I can remember. Last year there were so few apples, it wasn't worth pressing them. And you say, you are afraid so!

Marcel, don't play the fool! There's no way of fixing the papers if it's still in the vases.

The buggers even come in a snowstorm, whispered Emile.

We hide nothing, commanded Marcel.

Mathieu looked at him pityingly.

They came the day before yesterday, said the youngest assistant.

A car stopped on the bridge.

The buggers have come back again!

Two men got out, wearing city overcoats, spotless green wellington boots and, on their heads, tartan berets with woollen pompoms.

Good morning!

The chief inspector knew better than to hold out his hand. The younger one did so and nobody took it.

Gentlemen, boomed Emile, what have they always taxed? They tax whatever gives pleasure to the poor. Salt, tobacco, gnôle! the poor have no right to pleasures. If they had, it would discourage the rich!

The chief inspector deliberately ignored the old man. I don't suppose you expected us back so soon, he said to Mathieu.

There were thirty distilling engines in the region, and if the two inspectors did their rounds regularly, one could count on a month between visits.

It was the little question of the emergency tap which brought us back so soon.

The chief inspector spoke as if he were explaining to children, then, removing his gloves, he examined the tap of the serpentine condenser, put a finger to it and smelt the tip of his finger.

Old goat shit! muttered Emile.

The inspectors were like actors in a sinister theatre, sinister because everything they did was addressed to an authority who was not present.

You've drawn some off, said the inspector folding his arms across his chest.

What's been drawn off, said Marcel, nodding at his demijohns, is there!

Are they yours?

They are mine.

And the paper form?

The paper form is yours.

Have you filled it in?

How could I? I don't know how many litres my marc will yield yet.

Are all three vases yours?

Yes, they are mine.

They are going to make a little more than the statutory twenty litres, aren't they? The chief inspector smiled at the absent authority.

Mathieu pretended to study the dials of the boiler.

A good year for apples, said the young inspector, hoping to be affable.

The chief took a pen out of his pocket.

Do you know what this means? Marcel addressed the question as if to the snow. His gnôle was running out of the beak into the copper bucket which he had just emptied.

It means I'm going to have to pay, pay money for my own produce!

He spoke as solemnly and slowly as a priest saying a prayer over an open grave.

Marcel's marc yielded one hundred and sixty litres of eau-de-vie at fifty per cent, which meant that he had to pay on eighty-six litres the sum of two hundred and six thousand, four hundred francs: half the price of a four-year-old mare.

On his way home snow was blowing into Marcel's and Gui-Gui's eyes. He said afterwards that, as he rode in the cart, all explanations escaped him. All he could see was his next action drawing closer and becoming larger.

He unharnessed Gui-Gui and led her into the stable. The horse's stall, the large table in the kitchen, the ceiling-high cupboard where the gnôle bottle was kept, the cellar door—because the bottle was empty and he had to go and fill it from the demijohn—the wardrobe in the bedroom from which he took his shotgun, the bed on which he sat to change his boots, these wooden things, so solid to the touch, worn and polished, protected from the snow, placed in the house before he was born, built with wood that came from the forest which, through the window, was now no more than a darkness behind the falling snow, reminded him with a force, such as he had never experienced before, of all the dead who were his family and who had lived and worked in the same farm. He poured out a glass of gnôle for himself. The feeling came back into his feet. His ancestors were in the house with him.

At midday he was standing on the side of the road which led down from the hamlet where the distillers were still working. He had changed his leather jacket and wore an overcoat and cap. He waited for half an hour. For the Prosecution this half hour was to be proof that his action was premeditated.

At last a car came slowly round the corner. Standing in the middle of the road, Marcel waved his arms, the shotgun hidden under his overcoat. The car stopped.

The chief inspector wound down his snow-covered window.

What is it? he asked.

Marcel uncovered the barrels of his shotgun.

A good year for apples! he said.

The windscreen wipers stopped. There was only the sound of the engine ticking over.

Give me the ignition key. Thank you. Now ask your colleague to get out and stand by the headlights. Tell him to shut the door. Good. Wait a moment, let's see. He and I will get into the back of the car. And you will drive where I tell you.

This hold-up in the snow, said the chief inspector under cross-examination by the Prosecution, was as terrifying as an encounter with the Yeti.

The judge asked what a Yeti was. The Yeti is an anthropoid monster who lives in the Himalayas.

After a few minutes Marcel told the inspector to stop the car. The pine trees were weighed down with snow, and on the left of the road was a steep escarpment.

From here we walk, he said. Give me the key. Wait a moment, let's see. Yes, open the driver's door.

They took a path which led down the escarpment. Only Marcel

knew where the path led. His two prisoners fell, lost their gloves and floundered in the waist-high snow. To tell the truth, testified the younger one, the prospect of falling over the edge did not disturb me much because I was convinced anyway that we were being taken to our place of execution.

At the bottom of the escarpment there had once been a farm. It had burnt down and only the wooden grenier, the size of a horse's stall, remained.

Marcel handed the chief inspector a large key, as long as a hammer.

Open the bottom door.

The door was no taller than their chests. The inspectors had to stoop to enter. There were no windows. The floor was stone, and the wooden walls were as thick as the door. Greniers were built like strong-rooms.

What are you going to do? asked the chief inspector.

Now at last he did not speak for the benefit of the absent authority. He was addressing directly the man who held the gun and sat in the doorway.

I'm going to shut the door and lock it from the outside!

You can't do that. We'll freeze to death.

Marcel shook his head.

Our clothes are wet.

They'll dry.

There's no window. We'll die of suffocation.

The silhouette in the door again shook his head.

There's no light.

No, there's no light.

There'll be a search party out for us!

Not yet.

I tell you, if you leave us here, we'll die of exposure.

I'm leaving you a bottle of gnôle. Marcel stood the bottle on the floor.

How long? asked the chief.

Without answering Marcel got to his feet, went out into the snow and locked the door with the key. The inspectors, who belonged to the Special Section for the Investigation of Fraud of the Ministry of Finance, were thumping with their fists against the ceiling.

When Marcel reached the car on the road above, he hesitated. He tried to push it to the edge of the escarpment. His boots slipped in the snow. He knew enough about driving to drive ten metres. He had been right that it wouldn't have taken him long to learn to drive a tractor. Cautiously he got out of the driver's seat. This time he scarcely had to push. The car crept forward, and plunged down the shale slope. When it hit a pine tree it turned over and rolled further down. Finally it came to rest on its side and the snow started to cover it.

Is their car still there? he once asked Nicole when she came to visit him in the prison at B. . . .

Before nightfall he returned to the grenier. It stank of gnôle. The prisoners said they had knocked over the bottle in the dark. He suspected that they had drunk most of it, and then broken the bottle deliberately with the idea of using it as a cutting tool or a weapon. There was blood on the younger one's hand.

We use gnôle as an antiseptic, Marcel said. We also use it for preserving fruit and herbs so that we have something special to offer guests when they visit.

Our families will have notified the police, warned the chief inspector.

We use it too, continued Marcel, for dulling the pain of animals.

The chief had taken off his tartan cap and was using it as a kind of muff for his hands as he paced backwards and forwards. He could only take two very short strides in each direction.

To kidnap two state officials, said the chief inspector as he turned in circles, in pursuit of their official duty is an act of treason. You will be tried and sentenced. Make no mistake about it. They are already out looking for us!

Marcel sat in the doorway, the gun across his knees, studying his prisoners.

You have no hope of escape, said the chief inspector. The weight he was giving to each word, before his voice fell over it to proceed to the next, suggested that he was drunk.

Marcel stared at him, wondering.

Suddenly the chief inspector stopped turning in circles and knelt on the floor.

Listen, my friend, listen carefully to what I'm going to say now. Release us. Take us back to our car. I shall have to report the matter but we'll say it was a practical joke. Nothing more serious than a practical joke. We'll call it a joke! shall we call it a joke now?

The chief inspector held out his hand to clinch the deal.

I've brought you bread, water, two blankets, matches and a candle, said Marcel. The candle won't burn all night so you had better economise with it.

The chief inspector was on his feet, pacing in circles again. For the last time, he screamed at the top of his voice, we're offering to consider you a joker!

Marcel left them and hid the shotgun in the upper part of the grenier to save taking it home. It was freezing hard and his boots squeaked in the snow as he followed his own tracks and planned what to do next.

The same evening he visited his neighbour Jean-François. All the village knew by now that Marcel had had the bad luck to be booked by the inspectors. Jean-François commiserated with him. What has happened has happened, said Marcel. Nobody yet knew that the inspectors had disappeared. Marcel came quickly to the point of his visit.

I want to borrow six sheep.

In God's name what do you want them for?

For a practical joke.

On who?

I can't tell you.

On me?

No.

Jean-François started to laugh. If it's not on me, what are you going to do with the sheep? You're going to put them somewhere unlikely, aren't you? Somewhere where you never think of a sheep. In the Chapel? Seigneur! What an idea. You're going to take them to the Chapel!

I can't tell you!

How long do you want them for?

A few days.

A few days. It's a joke that goes on then?

It's a lesson—

A lesson! I see it now. You're going to take them to the school! You want them for several lessons. Why do you need six? Wouldn't one be enough?

I need six.

The following day Marcel fetched the sheep in his cart. A bluish frost settled on the curls of their grey wool, and they buried their muzzles in each other's flanks. When he turned round to look into the cart he saw only one anxiously raised head. The others were huddled together, heads down.

To cross the field to the grenier he had to carry the sheep on his shoulders one at a time. In the upper room of greniers were stored bottled fruit, honey, the bed linen, the wool, the wedding dress, the coverlet for the cradle; in the bottom room were stored sacks of flour and grain, purified butter, the bacon and the dem-ijohns of *gnôle*. Greniers were always built a certain distance from their farm so that if the house caught fire, the basic victuals and a few family treasures would be saved.

Marcel opened the bottom door. It smelt of urine. The two men hunched up against the far wall put their hands to their faces to protect their eyes against the sudden light.

You are moving upstairs, Marcel told them.

My colleague needs a doctor, said the young inspector. He has acute pains in his stomach.

He'll be more comfortable upstairs. Put your hands on your heads, both of you. Come on out! Let me see. Yes, go up the stairway on the left.

The two prisoners, having stooped to pass through the small door, did not bother to straighten their backs on the staircase, and climbed up on all fours. The younger one pushed open the upper door, and found himself staring into a ewe's eyes.

There's no room, he muttered, it's full of sheep.

They won't hurt you.

It's impossible! said the chief.

Marcel swore and jabbed his gun at him.

Bent double, the men entered and the sheep bleated.

There's a bale of straw in the corner, said Marcel.

His two prisoners sat on the bale. The sitting position made them less animal-like.

We can't survive another night here, said the chief inspector gravely. This is a form of torture to which you are subjecting us, you realise that, don't you?

That's why I brought the sheep. My grandmother used to say: It saves wood to sleep in the stable. She came from the other side of the mountains where there is no forest and wood is scarce.

We shivered all night, the young one said.

Tonight the sheep will warm you.

My colleague needs a doctor. He suffers from an ulcer, and has acute pains in his stomach.

There's bread and milk for you.

What are you going to do with us?

When you're ready to listen I'm going to talk.

Talk?

About justice.

Justice! yelled the chief inspector. The sheep turned their heads and looked at him with startled eyes. *You* are going to talk about justice! You'll soon be fleeing from justice!

The sheep kept turning in circles looking for a way out, and finding only the walls and the legs of the two seated prisoners. One of the sheep raised her tail to piss. Marcel, standing on the outside staircase, straightened his back so that his head was no longer visible from the inside of the room. It was as if the two men had already been left alone with the sheep and the fact that they were herded so closely together with these animals made their isolation sharper.

You are right, said the older inspector. Why not talk?

Marcel heard the remark but did not put his head back through the door.

Tell me, the inspector went on, how much are you asking for us? You may be asking an unrealistic sum—in which case we could help you.

Marcel bent his knees and looked again at his prisoners.

If you are asking a billion, it's too much. They won't pay that for us. Are you in touch with our families or the Ministry?

Marcel gave no sign of having heard the question.

We have a right to know. How much are you asking? Is it more than fifty million? I'd say fifty million is the maximum one could expect them to pay for men like us.

Despair, irreversible as the sound of an avalanche, suddenly engulfed Marcel.

If I'm asking too much, he spoke with his mouth almost shut, why do you care?

We are both married men with children. We are worried for our families.

Once again Marcel appeared not to have heard.

How much are you asking? insisted the chief inspector. You must understand that we have more experience than you of the value of money.

Marcel thrust his fists into the fleece of the nearest sheep and spoke as though to the animal. The value of money! he cried. The value of money!

The other three sheep raised their heads towards the wailing figure in the doorway and started to bleat. The value of money! The value of money! He grasped at the wool.

Slowly his fists relaxed. The sheep quietened. He looked at his two prisoners and spoke.

You are worried, he said. I regret to have to tell you that there is a tax to pay on worry! There's also a tax to pay on pain and a tax on shivering. A thousand francs a shiver! You say you both shivered all night? If only one of you had stayed warm, it would have saved you money! Still, tonight the sheep will save you hundreds of thousands. Last night, though, you are obliged to pay for! Have you filled in the form for your pain? You spoke of an ulcer, that's a sharp pain, and the sharper the pain, the higher the tax!

He has gone mad! The younger inspector took hold of the chief inspector's shoulders and began to shake him. Do something quick, he's gone out of his mind.

The chief inspector drew out his wallet and threw it over the backs of the sheep towards the peasant.

The wallet lay on the top step. Marcel put his boot on it, and turning his foot, pressed it, as if killing a salamander. Then he left without uttering a word.

He did not ride in the cart. He walked beside Gui-Gui. Walking is a form of thinking. After ten minutes he said to the horse:

It ends in defeat because you can only take revenge on those who are your own. Those two up there belong to another time. They are our prisoners and yet no revenge is possible. They would never know what we were avenging.

Next morning after he and Nicole had milked the cows, he stayed alone in the stable, as he did every morning, to brush and groom the animals until their haunches shone like polished walnut wood. Then he harnessed Gui-Gui to the cart and returned to the grenier.

The prisoners made no attempt to leave when he picked up a sheep and, leaving the door open, carried her away on his shoulders.

Why don't you go?

You have a gun.

I'm releasing you.

Why? asked the chief inspector suspiciously.

You do not have to know that too.

Backs bent to pass through the tiny door, the two men stepped outside and shielded their eyes with their hands from the sunshine coming off the snow. Their clothes were filthy. Their faces were creased and unshaven. They stood there, uncertain what to do next.

When the police handcuffed Marcel that afternoon the sky was blue and cloudless, the blue extending far beyond the furthest mountain. The snow on the peaks looked as innocent of the past as a baby after sleep.

He was charged with rebellion against officers of the state, armed robbery and the wilful destruction of public property. He served two months' preventive detention and, at his trial, was sentenced to two years' imprisonment.

In the prison at B . . . he looked at his hands which lay idle and heavy in his lap. What has been taken away from me, he said, is the habit of working. I will never again be able to load thirteen tipcarts and take Gui-Gui to the top field.

Hay

The flowers in her hair
wet in the morning
are dry by ten

Her apron clings
stones like hands
press in her pocket

Tomorrow
the scythes will gasp
as her clothes fall down

On this slope she'll lie
hands on its shoulder
feet on the road below

Gathered in lines
her cocks will crouch
like couples in the moonlight

Next day in the sun
she'll walk on her hands
to get as dry as fire

Combed by the women
lifted by men
she'll ride the carts

Front wheels locked
with a pole through their spokes
I'll take her down

And when I pack her
second wife under my roof
my sweat will blind me.

The Three Lives of
Lucie Cabrol

THE COCADRILLE WAS BORN in 1900 in the month of September. White cloud, like smoke, was blowing through the open door of the stable. Marius Cabrol was milking. His wife, Mélanie, was in bed, on the other side of the stable wall, attended by her sister and a neighbour. Their first child had been a boy, christened Emile. Marius, the father, hoped that the second would also be a son. He would be named Henri after his grandfather.

The Cabrol farm is on a slope above the village which is called Brine. On the south side of the house the ground flattens out and there are plum trees and a quince. Beside the house is a stream which Henri, the grandfather, channelled to drive a saw. If a log started to roll from up there, it wouldn't stop till it reached the church. I like to think of the logs I have rolled from high up! If the log is not straight, it leaps like an animal. You watch it from above and it is like an animal galloping. Gradually as the slope levels out, it slows down. When you expect it to lie still, it leaps again. It takes a long time for the flat ground to kill a rolling log.

On the bed Mélanie gripped the headboard. The water was already boiling on the stove in the kitchen. The baby was born very quickly. When I think of her being born, my mind wanders and I see her fishing. She was fourteen and I was three years older. She walked upstream, watching both banks. When she prodded with a stick under a stone, two dark shadows slipped across the river to the other bank. From that moment onwards she never shifted her gaze. She tucked her skirt into its own waist-band and without looking down for an instant she waded across. There she stood absolutely still. The water flowing round her thighs made the same noise as it does flowing round two small stationary rocks.

One of the trout left the overhanging bank and darted under a boulder. Was it because she was so small that she was so quick? Or was it because, being blind to warnings, she could read signs which are lost on others? Frisking under the boulder, she trapped the fish and pressed upwards with all the force of her small hand against the stone. The fish was fixed there like a long tongue. And, like a tongue, it tried to retract itself, reaching back down the throat of the water. It tried to thrust forward out of the throat. It tried to turn on its side. Slowly, never letting up the pressure of her palm, she inserted a tiny finger between tongue and stone and two more fingers between tongue and palm. All this with one hand. The instant he went still, she had him out of the water wedged between her three fingers, two with their backs to him.

It's a girl! cried the neighbour.

La Mélanie looked tenderly, and with surprise, at the tiny body, the colour of a radish, held upside down.

Give her to me.

On the forehead of the baby's puckered face was a dark, red mark.

Jésus! Forgive me! La Mélanie screamed. She is marked with the mark of the craving.

When a woman is pregnant, she sometimes craves for something special to eat or drink or touch. It is the right of the mother, by a kind of decree of nature, to have what she wants. Yet often it is not possible, and it is then that she must be careful. For if one of her cravings is denied, the next time she touches her body, the touch may be printed in the same place on the embryo in her womb. And so it is better when one of her cravings has been unsatisfied, for her to touch deliberately her foot or her bottom: otherwise, without thinking, she may touch her cheek or her ear and this will be printed as a disfiguring mark on the child.

Jésus! cried La Mélanie again. I have marked her face with the mark of the craving.

Mélanie, be calm. It is not the mark of the craving. I've seen it often. It is where her face rubbed as she came out, said her sister.

The neighbour took the baby to press the top of her head so that it should be as round as possible.

It was when I wanted to eat freshwater fish! La Mélanie insisted.

Her sister was proved right, for in a few days the red mark disappeared, and only much later did La Mélanie ask herself whether her daughter had not, after all, been marked by the mark of another kind of craving. As a young child, two things were unusual about her. She remained very small. And as soon as she could crawl, and later walk, she had a habit of disappearing.

You lose her as easily as you lose a button, La Mélanie said.

I think of Lucie—for that is how she was christened—as a baby in her cradle. What is the difference between a baby and a small animal? An animal goes straight along its own path. A baby vacillates, rolling first to one side and then to the other. Either she's all smiles and gurgles, or a face all puckered up and bawling.

When she was six, Lucie was missing for a whole day. If I go out of the door now and take a few steps up the hillside to where the cows are grazing, I can see the track she took.

It leads to the skyline where the moon rises. In August when the cows are grazing up there, they are silhouetted as if against a great circular lantern. From there the path leads along the crest to a pass where there are some marmots, through a moraine of boulders the size of houses, along the edge of an escarpment, and finally down to the forest below.

In the evening Lucie came back with her hat full of mushrooms. Yet by that time, Marius à Brine had organised a search-party. I remember the men filling their lamps with paraffin.

When there wasn't any work to be done at home, Lucie went to school. The village teacher was called Masson. He used to read from the *Life of Voltaire* and the curé preached against this book in church. One thing impressed me about the *Life of Voltaire*. When there was famine, he distributed sacks of grain among the peasants at Ferney. Otherwise, the *Life of Voltaire* belonged to that collection of books which we knew existed and which entailed a way of life we could not imagine. At what time of day did people read? we asked ourselves.

Masson was killed at Verdun. His name is on the war memorial. Each morning, before the first lesson began, he wrote on the blackboard the day of the week, the date of the month and the year of the century. On the war memorial there is only the month and the year of his death: March 1916. After the date each morning, he wrote a saying on the blackboard which we children copied into our books:

Insults should be written on sand
Compliments should be inscribed on marble.

It was in her last year at school that Lucie was given the nickname of the Cocadrille. A *cocadrille* comes from a cock's egg hatched in a dung heap. As soon as it comes out of its egg, it makes its way to the most unlikely place. If it is seen by somebody it has not seen, it dies. Otherwise, it can defend itself and can kill anything it chooses, except the weasel. The poison, with which it kills, comes from its eyes and travels along its gaze.

Soon after Lucie was born, La Mélanie had another son who was christened Henri. By the time he was two, he was larger than his sister who could by then sit on the horse, fetch wood for the stove and feed the chickens. It could be that her tiny size was a kind of provocation to jealousy. Small children normally accord rights according to size. Whatever the reason, Henri hated his sister. It was he who, forty years later, said to the Mayor: This sister has never brought anything but shame to our family.

One day Mélanie found three of her chickens dead. The killer was not a fox or a weasel, for the chickens were untouched.

Lucie killed them! shouted Henri, she looked at them and they died.

I never touched them!

She's a Cocadrille!

I'm not! I'm not!

The Cocadrille! The Cocadrille! shouted Henri.

Stop your bickering, the mother grumbled.

That time the nickname did not stick. The next time it did.

It was between Easter and Whitsun. Later, when I was in the Argentine, I used to tell myself that I could not die until I had seen another month of May, here in the mountains. The grass grows knee-high in the meadows and down the centre of the roads between the wheel ruts. If you are with a friend, you walk down the road with the grass between you. In the forest the late beech leaves come out, the greenest leaves in the world. The cows are let out of the stable for the first time. They leap, kick with their hind legs, turn in circles, jump like goats. The month itself is like a home-coming.

Her brother Emile had left in the autumn to work in Paris as a stoker for the central heating of the new department store of Samaritaine. La Mélanie could not read the postcard which had come, so she gave it to Lucie.

Emile's coming home!

When?

Sunday.

On the Friday Marius chose the largest of his black rabbits, and, holding it up by its ears, he felt its flesh through the fur.

Yes, you big crook, Emile is coming home!

He stroked it again and then knocked it unconscious with one blow. Delicately, he cut out its two eyes. Their lashes remained unhurt round the two holes through which the blood flowed when he hung it up by its hind legs to bleed. On Sunday morning Mélanie skinned it and cooked it in cider.

Emile's present for Lucie was a silver-painted model of the Eiffel Tower.

Did you see it? she asked in excitement.

You see it everywhere. It's three hundred metres high.

At the end of the meal La Mélanie collected up in her hands the neat piles of bones laid on the table beside each plate. The rabbit bones were so clean they looked as if they were made from horn or ivory on which there had never been meat. She was happy. Her son who had come home was already asleep in his room.

Each evening Henri and Lucie took the milk down to the dairy. Lucie's size never affected her strength. She was as tough as a mountain goat. The same as Henri, she carried twenty litres on her back, the can strapped on like a school satchel. That evening, after he had slept, Emile said he would go with them.

Give me the milk, Lucie.

She refused. Her head was scarcely higher than Emile's waist.

Could you find me a job in Paris? she asked.

You could work in a baker's.

Do you live in the same place as you work?

I catch the Métro. The Métro is a train, an electric train that goes underground . . .

What time do the trains start in the morning? asked Henri.

Early, but the Parisians can't get out of bed. So they're always in a hurry. You should see them running along the tunnels to catch the trains.

The trains don't stop? asked the Cocadrille.

The path down to the village followed a stream and near the bottom was a lilac tree. When the lilac was in flower, you could smell the tree thirty metres away.

Tell me more about Paris.

People sleep in the streets, said Emile.

Why?

If they asked for shelter, the Parisians would never let them come in.

Why don't they build sheds?

There is no wood to build with.

No trees?

It's forbidden.

Do you know what Grandfather Revuz did? Lucie asked. The Mayor told him he couldn't cut down an acacia. And he cut it down. After he cut it down, he said the leaves on that bush were too small for him to wipe his arse on! And if they were that small, he said, it couldn't have been an acacia.

Grandfather Revuz may think he's clever but he'd be lost in Paris, said Emile. Do you know how many horses there are there?

Fifty thousand! guessed Henri.

Two million, said Emile with pride.

Will you take me with you next time? Lucie asked.

They would lock you up! said Henri.

When they went into the dairy, the cheesemaker straightened his back, extended a hand and shouted:

So 'Mile is back from Paris!

For the summer.

How old are you now?

Sixteen, Emile replied.

Never too young!

The cheesemaker, whose wife cuckolded him regularly, winked.

Henri and Lucie unstrapped their cans. In the middle of the dairy a cauldron hung from its wooden gallows. The dairy was well-placed because it was cool even in summer. The cheesemaker's wife complained that her husband's feet were perpetually like ice.

Did you climb to the top? Lucie asked Emile.

What top?

The top of the Eiffel Tower!

You go up by a lift, Emile said.

Lift?

Yes, lift.

What's a lift? she asked.

The Cocadrille knows nothing, roared Henri, laughing. The proper place for her is her dung heap.

None of them was looking at her. She removed the lid of her milk can. She picked it up and, as you throw water out of a bucket, she hurled litres of milk into Henri's face. Whilst the milk was dripping from his hair, she screamed:

If you weren't a weasel I'd kill you!

The cheesemaker, swearing, tried to hit her, but she escaped, ran round the cauldron and vanished out of the door.

The story soon reached the ears of Marius à Brine. He found his daughter by the washing trough and he started to beat her, shouting:

Milk is not water! Milk is not water!

After a few blows he stopped. She was staring at him with her bright blue eyes. She had eyes the colour of forget-me-nots. Her look forced him to gather her into his arms and to press her face against his stomach.

Ah! My Cocadrille. You came out like that, didn't you? You can't help it. You just came out like that.

She stepped with her small feet onto his boots and then he carried her on his feet across the yard, repeating and laughing: The Cocadrille! The Cocadrille!

And so the name Cocadrille, born of both hatred and love, replaced the name Lucie. When she was thirteen, a circus came to the village and put up its tent in the square. The circus consisted of one family, a goat which could stand on the smallest milking-stool we ever saw, and two ponies. The father was ringmaster, the mother was acrobat and their son was the clown. During the afternoon the son went round the cafés of the village and blew a trumpet to announce the evening performance. The men smiled at the trumpet but they did not invite him to drink, lest he make fun of them.

The circus also had an elephant. The elephant was a piece of grey cloth with a trunk sewn onto it. When the ringmaster turned to the benches where the kids were sitting and asked for volunteers, I rushed forward. I was the front of the elephant, and Joset, who was killed in an avalanche, was the back. Together we danced to an accordion which the clown was playing.

And now for a cow elephant! shouted the ringmaster, holding up a second piece of grey cloth. Two pretty girls please! The second piece of cloth had a pearl necklace painted on it, and from the huge folds of its ears hung a pair of earrings painted gold. The rings had been taken from a horse's bit.

The girls were all too shy. Not one put up her hand. I lifted up the cloth of the elephant's head and, facing the girls, cried out:

The Cocadrille! The Cocadrille! The Cocadrille!

And she came! Everyone in the tent clapped and laughed at the tiny figure who was going to be part of an elephant.

I heard the ringmaster whisper to his son:

She's a dwarf. Find out her age.

For a moment the Cocadrille stood there alone, eyes alight. Finally another girl climbed over the benches and joined her. Beside the Cocadrille, the other girl looked like a giant. The clown began to play music—a violin this time. The only way the Cocadrille could manage was to be the back of the elephant, and instead of bending forward at the waist, she stayed upright and pulled hard at the grey cloth so that it didn't sag in the middle of the animal's back. There we were, two elephants, a bull and a cow, with the violin playing.

There were pictures of elephants in our schoolbooks, because, from Hannibal to Napoleon, foreign generals had the idea of using elephants to cross the mountains. The four of us danced in the middle of the arena, and every time we stopped, the ringmaster cracked his whip over us, and the crowd shouted: Again! Again! Sometimes I caught sight of the Cocadrille's bare feet—she had kicked off her sabots—dancing jerkily at the back of the grey cow elephant.

Eventually they let us go. The clown son whispered something to the Cocadrille and then shook his head at his father, who shrugged his shoulders.

When I saw her next at school I asked her what she had thought of the circus. She didn't mention the dance of the elephants. What she liked, she said, was the clown on stilts. Could I make her a pair? I said I would.

I never made them. More than fifty years later she said to me— her eyes were stone-coloured by then—If I had a pair of stilts, I could cross the valley in ten strides. This was at the time when she was walking a hundred kilometres a week. Ten strides! she repeated.

The Cabrol farm at Brine is on the *advet,* the slope facing south. Opposite on the *ubac,* facing north, is a hamlet called Lapraz. There is a song about the cocks in each hamlet. The one at Lapraz, where there is less sun, calls out:

> I sing when I can.

The cock at Brine crows:

> I sing when I want!

To this the *ubac* cock replies:

> Then be content!

It was on the slope facing Lapraz in August 1914 that the Cabrol family were scything their patch of oats when they heard the church bell ringing in the valley below.

The war has started, said Marius.

The massacre of the world has begun, said La Mélanie.

Women usually know better than men the extent of catastrophe. The Mayor delivered the mobilisation papers. Most of those called up were in high spirits. Never again, not once, were the cafés in the village to be so full as on the evening before the mobilised men left. Marius, older than most of the others—he was thirty-eight—was apprehensive. He avoided the cafés and spent the evening at home, giving instructions to Emile about what had to be done before the snow came, by which time he would be back, and the war would be over.

The band played as the men marched out of the village along the road which followed the river to the plain. The band was smaller than usual, for half its players were among the soldiers who were leaving. I had joined the band the previous autumn and I was the youngest drummer.

Marius did not come back before the snow came, nor before the New Year, nor before the spring. The endless time of war began. The seasons changed, the years passed and all our lives, except those of the youngest children, who remembered nothing else, were in abeyance. Early in 1916 Emile and I were called up. Between young boys and old men there was nobody left. There were no full male voices to be heard. The horses became accustomed to the commands of women.

La Mélanie, the Cocadrille and Henri ran the farm. There was so much to be done that the younger brother could not afford to quarrel openly with his sister. If Henri made the Cocadrille angry, she would disappear for the rest of the day, and he realised that they could not do without her labour even for a few hours.

Despite her size, she was tireless. She was like the small humming-bird who, when the time comes to migrate, can fly a thousand miles across the Bay of Mexico. She was not the second woman of the house, she was more like a hired hand—a man. A midget man with a difficult and unpredictable character. She drove the mare, she fetched wood, she led the horse when Henri ploughed, she fed the cows, she dug the garden, she made the cider, she preserved the fruit, she mended the harnesses. She never washed clothes nor sewed. In a *pailler* on top of her head she could carry eighty kilos of hay. If you saw her from behind, it looked like magic: the linen tent, full of hay, completely hid her and so it appeared to be moving down the slope, alone, on its lowermost corner. Both La Mélanie and Henri were somewhat frightened of her when she sat with them in the kitchen. They never knew how she could take what was said.

At the beginning of 1918 the family at Brine received a telegram informing them that Emile had been gravely wounded near Compiègne. Each evening the Cocadrille asked the milk, frothing in the wooden bucket, to keep her brother Emile alive.

He stayed alive and after months in hospital came home. When at last Marius too returned, Mélanie saw that her son now looked older than his father. Nobody in the village spoke of victory, they only spoke of the war being ended.

A year after his demobilisation Marius announced to Emile that La Mélanie was expecting another baby.

At her age! said Emile.

Marius nodded: It will be our last.

It will have to be!

The more scandalised the son's expression, the more the father smiled.

All the war I promised myself that.

And Mother?

I survived.

So we'll be four, concluded Emile.

He meant that the family inheritance would be divided into four.

Yes, if you count the Cocadrille.

Have you told the Cocadrille?

Not yet.

I wonder how she will take it.

It's for Mother to tell her.

It'll change the Cocadrille.

How is that?

It will change her. Me and the Cocadrille, we might be married now with our own children. Yet who is going to marry the Cocadrille? And I'm too sick to marry. It ought to be our turn and, instead, you've made another baby.

Call it an old man's last sin! Marius, however penitent, could not stop smiling.

In December 1919 La Mélanie's last baby was born and was

christened Edmond. I stayed in the army an extra year to learn mechanics. I came back to the village at the beginning of 1920.

The following June, four men took the steep path, up to the alpage. They were young and they climbed quickly. With them they carried an accordion, eight loaves of bread and a sack of coarse salt for the cattle. They had worked all day and it was beginning to become dusk.

At one point where the cumin grows profusely either side of the path, the one who was leading stopped and all four looked down at the village, seven hundred metres below.

You can see André's sheep, Robert said.

They could also see the road out of the village which followed the river and led to the plain.

He's slow, is André.

He slowed down ever since the death of Honorine.

He should marry again.

Who?

Philomène!

They laughed and looked down on the village, with the assurance of youth: an assurance which comes from the conviction that, because the young see clearly, they will avoid the mistakes of the old.

Philomène has driven stronger men than André out of the house!

Out of their minds!

When they arrived at the top, the pastures were full of small birds flying just above the grass. The flight of these birds is like a line of stitches, they beat their wings as fast as butterflies and with this they gain height; then they glide and lose height till they beat their wings again and begin another stitch. As they fly they chirp making a noise like castanets.

These birds, flying at the level of their hands, made the men think of the eyes and names of the girls they had come to visit. Very soon the birds would stop flying and night fall.

From time to time a visiting archprêtre would preach a sermon against the immorality of leaving young women alone in the alpage. Our own curé knew that there was no alternative. It was the unmarried daughter, capable of looking after the cows and making the cheese, who had the pair of hands most easily spared from the work below. Old women still talk of their summers in the alpage.

Before making their visits that night, the four young men planned to sing. There is a place surrounded on three sides by a rock which resounds like the choir of a church. There they were going to sing to announce their arrival to the young women whom they had already, in imagination, chosen. Yet for their singing to be a surprise, they had to skirt the main group of chalets and reach the horseshoe of rocks unseen. This detour involved passing only one chalet, which was unimportant, because it was the Cocadrille's.

As the four approached, the Cocadrille came to her doorway. What emphasised her smallness was the fact that, although she wore the clothes of a woman, she had neither hips nor bust. She had the figure of the ideal servant, tiny but active, without age or sex. That summer she was twenty.

You have an accordion, she said.

Yes, we have.

I can dance, she replied.

Not in those sabots, you can't!

She kicked them off, just as she had kicked them off when she was dancing at the back of the elephant. Her feet were black with dirt. Without waiting for the music, she began to lift up her knees and to step ferociously on the earth around the entrance to the stable where the coming and going of the cows had already worn away the grass. Just by dancing she forced Robert to play a few chords.

Stop! I shouted. The music will tell the others we're here.

The music of the accordion died down. The Cocadrille looked straight at me, unblinking, and slipped her feet back into her clogs. What was disconcerting about her look was its fixity. It was as if her head and neck became suddenly paralysed.

We must be on our way.

Can one of you help me move a barrel? she asked. Robert stepped forward.

Not you, she said, better the one who has just come back from the army.

I shrugged my shoulders and asked my three companions to wait.

Let them go, she said.

Guffawing and making signs with their hands, they left.

Tell La Nan I'm coming to visit her! I shouted after them.

The barrel had oil for the lamp in it. After I had shifted it, the Cocadrille offered me coffee. At first I could hardly see inside the chalet. I stood there, holding the cup in my hands, and she poured gnôle into it without asking. To pour gnôle into my cup she had to raise her arm higher than her shoulder.

You'd be small enough for a chimney-sweep, I said, not knowing what else to say.

I'm a woman, she replied, and I'd shit down their chimneys.

In the very dim light which made her almost invisible, her voice sounded like a woman's.

Are you going away to work in Paris this autumn? she asked.

Yes.

I'll catch a marmot for you to take with you.

How?

That's my secret.

You dig them up when they're asleep?

Will you go up the Eiffel Tower? she asked, ignoring my remark.

The others will be waiting, I said. Thank you for the coffee.

They're singing, she told me. Can't you hear?

No.

She opened the door. They were singing "Mon père a cinq cent moutons."

I'll fetch you some butter, she said.

We don't need any.

You have so much at home that you can refuse butter?

She left me and went through the door into the stable. By now the moon was up, and a little of its light came through the dusty window, no larger than an open book, and down the wooden chimney. There was a pool of moonlight around the dead ashes.

When the Cocadrille came back, I gasped. She had taken off her blouse and chemise. I could see her breasts, each scarcely larger than the bowl of a wooden spoon. She came and stood right in front of me, and I saw that the dark nipples of her breasts were dripping with milk.

It was not until next morning that I reasoned that she must have poured cow's milk over her breasts when she went into the stable. At the time I thought of nothing beyond the thin warm arms she put round me.

We went to lie on the bed, a wooden shelf at the far end of the room. As I caressed her, lying on the bed, I had the impression that she grew larger. She grew as large as the earth upon which I had to throw myself.

How you stir me! she cried, you stir my milk!

The only other time I had been to bed with a woman was in a brothel in the garrison town of L . . . , and there the lights were pink and the prostitute was as white and plump as a pig. Was that, I asked myself later, why the Cocadrille had asked for the one who had been in the army?

At two in the morning she dressed and reminded me not to forget the butter. As I left, she reached up and pulled the hair at the back of my head, digging her nails into my scalp. I knew the path down by heart.

Suddenly a cloud obscured the moon so that I could see nothing. A noise in the undergrowth made me stop. On every side the low bushes were being trampled. For the third or fourth time that night my heart raced wildly, yet this time, unlike the others, my whole body felt icy. I took to my heels. I ran for ten minutes without stopping, as if I were running from damnation itself.

Later when I reasoned that the Cocadrille must have poured cow's milk over her breasts, I also reasoned that on my way home I had disturbed some sleeping goats.

What was it that made me go back the following evening? Why did I deliberately go up alone, avoiding my companions? She gave no sign of surprise at my arrival.

So you've finished the butter! she said.

Can you give me some more?

Yes, Jean. She pronounced my name solemnly in her deep voice. It was as if she had invented the name herself. Nobody else had ever said my name like that. It disturbed me because it separated me from all other men called Jean or Théophile or François.

She made some coffee. I asked her what she had done and she recounted her day to me. She asked me nothing about myself, but sometimes she looked at me, as if to make sure that I corresponded with the name she had pronounced. We sat across the table, facing each other in the darkness. It was now as dark outside as in. There would be lights in the windows of the other chalets. I knew why she had not lit the lamp: any visitor would conclude that she was already asleep. When a cow moved her head in the stable the note of the bell filled the room, and it was like a reminder of what we were about to do. By now neither of us spoke. I could even hear the breath of the cows. It crossed my mind to leave then and there. Yet it was already too late. Everything outside was already distant, like a coastline seen from the stern of a ship.

She had placed a candle by the bed. Without a word, she lit it. The blanket was white and smelt of sunlight. In the morning, after the cows had grazed, she must have washed the blood from the blanket. I lay there and watched her undress. She threw her clothes onto the table and strode onto the bed.

Stir me! She said this standing over me.

I began to shout at her. I called her obscene names. I referred to parts of her with the words we used for animal parts. All she did was to smile and then, squatting, she sat on me as if I were a horse. I tried to make her fall off and she held onto my shoulders and laughed. Her laughing made me laugh. My shouting stopped. I made a noise like a horse neighing. I neighed and she gripped the hair above my ears as if it were a mane. Later I asked myself how she made me do such things.

We played and made love on the wooden stage of the bed as though we possessed the strength of the whole village. Perhaps that is an old man's boast. I could literally pick her up with one arm, yet every time I tried to put my feet on the floor, she succeeded in pulling me back. It was difficult to believe she was the same woman whom I had passed so often, during the first years of the war, working alone in a field, cursing and already bent with a kind of weariness. I made her laugh by measuring her limb by limb, part by part, against myself. Today I have made a mark on the doorpost of the kitchen to help me recall her real height, before, like all of us, she shrank in old age. One metre, twenty-five centimetres is what I've marked. None of the rest is measurable.

At last we were exhausted and I got up to breathe a little in the fresh air. On the slope behind the Cabrol chalet there is a fold in the earth like a furrow, down which a trickle of water runs. The water makes the flowers grow profusely there, and on both sides of the fold, there are millions of ranunculi, the small, white five-petalled flowers which cows will not eat. I sat down amongst these flowers and the Cocadrille, wearing a man's hat, came out to join me. The other chalets were silent. The crickets had long since stopped. Below were the roofs of the village, no larger than dice.

She lay back among the grasses and ranunculi and looked up at the sky where the stars were the same shape as the flowers, and lying on her back she began to talk. She spoke about herself, about her brother Emile, about the land she would one day inherit, about the cows, about what she thought of the curé, about how she would never marry. At first I listened to what she was saying without much attention. Then gradually it occurred to me that she was saying all this because it might turn out to be otherwise. I became convinced that she was plotting one thing whilst talking about its opposite. It wasn't true that she would never marry. She was plotting to make me her husband. She believed she was now pregnant and so I would be forced to marry her.

Lucie! I interrupted her as we sat there in the firmament of flowers. I do not know why I used her real name.

Yes?

I'm not going to come up again.

I didn't expect you to, Jean.

Her reply confirmed my worst suspicions. It meant that I was already trapped.

Here's the butter, she said, and the way she looked so fixedly at me scared me, making me feel alone and separate, as I had felt when I first arrived and she had used my name in such a strange way.

The next night, asleep in the bed with my brother, I dreamt of her. The Cocadrille came to the house, fearless, eyes blazing. Only one man can be the father of my child, she said in my dream, and Jean is that man! Is it true? asked my own father, turning to me. I couldn't answer. With the Cocadrille! he shouted. No, I don't believe it, he roared. I can prove it, she said. Then prove it! ordered my father. I counted the moles on the small of his back, said the Cocadrille. How many are there? my mother asked. The Cocadrille said a number, and I was forced to take down my trousers in front of the three of them whilst my father counted the moles. You've ruined your life, said my father. Ruined it for nothing! The number was correct. I woke up frightened and sweating.

Many times that summer I was tempted in the evenings to climb up to the alpage to discover whether or not she was pregnant. Each time I told myself it was better not. And so I stayed below in suspense. Finally, late in August, I saw her outside the church at a wedding and, to my great relief, she did not single me out in any way.

After I had been in Paris for two winters, Marius à Brine fell sick. It was the month of July and I was back in the village. La Mélanie sat by her husband's bed, lending him what courage she could, and the Cocadrille climbed up to the alpage to fetch ice to lay on his burning stomach. There is a cave there, near the horseshoe of rocks where the four of us were going to sing, into which the sun never penetrates. She filled a can with this broken ice, covered it with a shawl, and ran back all the way down to Brine. It was the same path I ran down that first night when I fled from the goats. By the time she arrived, more than half the ice had melted and there were only rounded slivers left to put on his pain-clenched stomach. She made three such journeys up to the cave, and when she came back the third time, in the mid-afternoon, Marius was dead.

I went to pay my last respects to him. He was laid out in his black suit and boots. At the foot of the bed the Cabrol family kept vigil. The Cocadrille was wearing a widow's dress like her mother and her face was inclined and invisible. I made the sign of the cross with the sprig of boxwood over his still heart and his head with its closed eyes. Edmond, his youngest son, was only three years old.

Food and drink were laid out for the visitors. The Cocadrille left the room of the dead and came out to offer me some apple rissoles. As I ate, she looked up at me. In her drawn, tearstained face, framed in black, her blue eyes were even more intense than I recollected. In April the first forget-me-nots appear in the grass, like flakes fallen from the sky. Dug up with their roots and brought inside the house they bring fine weather with them. Her eyes were the same blue.

So you are leaving us again? she said.

Yes. Not just for Paris, I'm going to South America.

Come back before you die, she said in her deep voice.

Her saying this angered me. I offered my condolences once more and left. After her father's death the Cocadrille continued to work on the farm.

In 1936 Emile died as the final consequence of his war wounds. Two years later La Mélanie followed her husband and her eldest son into the grave. Henri married Marie, a woman from the next village. The Cocadrille milked the cows, looked after the stable, grew the vegetables, collected wood, grazed the cattle. Marie, her sister-in-law, complained about her:

She's as dirty as a chicken house. And she never lifts a finger in the kitchen. What sort of woman is that?

The years passed. The Second War broke out.

One morning the Cocadrille was scything between the apple trees with her own scythe which she would never allow anyone else to touch. Over the years its blade had been worn down by whetting and beating until it was scarcely wider than a thumbnail. If you gave me the money, I could never buy another like this, she said. Only the work of twenty summers can make a scythe as light as this. For twenty summers I've cherished this scythe like a son. She was by now known for her original way of talking.

The air was still cooler than the earth under the grass. Far above the orchard, the forest was not yet in the full light of day. Looking up, the Cocadrille saw two men beckoning her from the edge of the trees. Her brothers noticed that she had stopped working and followed her gaze. The two strangers at the edge of the forest must have seen what they took to be a child and two peasants in a hayfield pointing towards them. This was in 1944.

Shit! said Henri.

They're maquisards, said Edmond, who was now as large as a man and already had a knowing expression.

What else could they be? grumbled Henri.

Jésus! don't let anyone else see them.

The Cocadrille pretended to have noticed nothing. It was always Edmond who spoke and Henri who waited, and then it was Henri who prided himself on his cunning.

Marie can give them food and they can go, said Henri after a long pause.

One of the two unknown men started down the slope. Halfway, he emerged from the shadow of the mountain and entered the early morning sunshine. He was short and burly and walked like a peasant.

The two brothers stood absolutely still lest any movement be interpreted by the stranger as a welcome. When he was a few metres away, the stranger said, Good morning.

In the fields deliberate silence is a powerful weapon. Henri said nothing, and withdrew his head back into his shoulders like a dog guarding a doorway. Edmond stood with his hands on his hips, staring insolently.

Two of us need shelter for twenty-four hours, announced the stranger, after allowing the silence to continue long enough to show that he had recognised it.

Who told you to come to our farm?

Nobody. We know who not to go to.

In God's name! muttered Henri. He took out his scythe stone and began sharpening the blade. The noise of the stone on the metal, like the previous silence, was intended to indicate a further refusal to answer.

The stranger strolled over towards the small figure who was still scything between the apple trees.

Good morning, little girl, he said to the Cocadrille.

She turned towards him and he saw that she was a middle-aged woman with a lined face, old enough to be his mother.

I didn't see . . . he excused himself.

This is also my farm, she said.

The stranger made a sign to his companion up by the forest. The second man was limping and carried a gun in each hand.

The two brothers, anxious to prevent the Cocadrille talking to the maquisard, came over to the apple trees.

Where are you from? Edmond asked.

I'm from the Dranse. The SS burnt down my father's farm there.

So you have nothing to lose? remarked Edmond.

Nothing.

The single word contained a threat. This time the silence was filled only with the gasp of the Cocadrille's scythe as it cut the grass.

We'll give you food and after that you must go, announced Henri.

No, we need to stay till tomorrow.

The man who limped and carried the guns joined them. He was young and his unshaven face looked worn and pain-filled.

The best way to hide, said Henri slyly, is to work with us. We need to get the hay in.

The comrade here has a wound that needs dressing, said the peasant from the Dranse.

We are not a hospital!

The Cocadrille leant on her scythe and looked across at the young man. Where is your wound? she asked.

The right thigh, he said.

I will dress it for you.

And if the Germans come? Henri yelled. He can't be in the house.

You are right, interrupted the peasant from the Dranse. It's better if we stay up here.

You mean the Germans *are* looking for you? said Edmond quickly.

Probably.

You came here with a wounded man and with the Germans on your heels and you expect us to risk our lives saving you!

They could hide in the chicken house.

No, we are safer, like you said, working with you. We are your cousins come to help with the hay. Is there anyone down there in the house?

My wife.

So you are four.

With the Cocadrille here, yes.

Can you, Madame, fetch hot water and bandages? Meanwhile we'll hide the weapons.

When she returned from the farm with some strips of linen sheet, she led the wounded man to a flat step of ground by the side of the stream which her grandfather had used to drive the saw. The wound near the top of his thigh was like a wound of any generation.

She knelt in her black dress by his hips and bent over the wound whilst she bathed it with hot water. It took her a long time to get the old dressing completely off. The wound was as red as beef. She diluted some *gnôle* and dabbed it on the wound. When it hurt him, his hand, lying on the grass, found her calf and gripped it through her dress.

Thank you, he said when at last she had bound the wound up again. You have very gentle hands.

Laid out on the grass, his body looked long and his bare legs as thin as those of the body on the cross.

Gentle! she said. They've worked too hard to be gentle. They've been in too much shit.

He shut his eyes.

How old are you? she asked.

Nineteen.

Is your mother alive?

I believe so.

And your father?

He is a judge.

You have such regular teeth. You don't come from here.

No, from Paris.

Have you ever turned hay?

I will do as you do.

She helped him to his feet. After a while, he stopped to wipe his face with the corner of his shirt.

She held out a bottle to him. However much you drink when haymaking, she said, you never piss!

At midday a car drew up at the farmhouse.

Take no notice, ordered the peasant from the Dranse, go on working.

Two men in uniform got out of the car.

They're not the Milice, said Edmond, they're Germans.

The Cocadrille, who was standing beside the young man from Paris, suddenly reached up and slapped the side of his neck with her open hand.

What! he shouted.

A horsefly had been about to bite him.

Soon they could hear the heavy breathing of the Germans whom the slope still hid from view. The first to appear was an officer with a tight belt and straight high cap, pulled down over his eyes. Following him came a sergeant holding a submachine-gun.

Everyone here! shouted the officer. He surveyed the five hay-makers: four peasants and one dwarf woman.

We are looking for six assassins. We know who they are. Who has come by here this morning?

I'll tell you, said the Cocadrille. The brain needs renewing. It wanders. If I had the money to buy a new one and if they sold them, I'd change it tomorrow. She buttoned her dress where it was undone. I did see a car go by this morning—or was it yesterday morning? An army could go by and I wouldn't be sure. When I saw this car I said to myself, that's strange. There was an officer driving it, with a cap like yours, sir—she pointed the prongs of her wooden fork at the officer's face: the sergeant pushed her back. I said to myself, he looks like a man wearing a disguise. Perhaps he was one of the men you are looking for, sir, one of the assassins.

His cap came right down over his face like yours, sir, as if he was trying to hide his face. Was it this morning or yesterday morning I saw this car? He could have stolen the car, you see, sir. Was it yesterday? I wish I knew. She put a finger in her ear. You'll do better, believe me, sir, asking my two cousins here. She pointed her fork at the maquisards.

Nobody's passed this way, said the peasant from the Dranse. Not since before it was light. We were up at five. Nobody has come by, unless they stuck to the forest and we didn't see them.

The peasant from the Dranse stared vacantly at the distant snow-covered mountain, white like a pillow propped against the blue sky, and farted.

The officer approached Edmond and gently touched his face so that he could look into the boy's eyes.

They couldn't come here, said Edmond ingratiatingly, they know too well where our sympathies lie.

No, the officer said, you all hate us!

And you? demanded the sergeant, pointing his gun at the young Parisian.

The hay is dry now. He spoke slowly and stupidly as if he were the dwarf woman's son.

What have you seen this morning?

Flies and horseflies.

Has anyone come down from the forest?

Flies and horseflies.

His idiocy provoked the sergeant to jab the muzzle of his gun hard into his stomach. The dwarf woman raised her fork in protest. The officer scowled at the prospect of a brawl on the steep slope which the hay made slippery.

We are wasting our time, he said curtly to the sergeant. To the peasants he said: If you are lying, I can promise you we'll be back, just as we came back to T . . .

The previous winter the Germans had come one night to the village of T . . . with two armoured lorries, an officer's car and a searchlight mounted on a sidecar. With their searchlight trained on the doors, they went from house to house. The women they chased into the forest. The men they lined up and shot. Whilst the stables and animals were burning, the German troops sang.

The sergeant left first. The officer, as he went down, dug his heels in so as not to slip, and the dust from the hay coated the backs of his polished boots.

After the car had driven away, there was nowhere any sign of what had happened or of what might happen.

The Aunt here made a fine speech! said the peasant from the Dranse. She scowled in case he was taking her for a fool. During her first life the Cocadrille was never indifferent to what people thought of her.

It's safe now. They won't come back until they've questioned everybody, she said to the one she had bandaged. You can go and rest in the hayloft.

He must work, Henri contradicted, that was the understanding from the beginning. If they come back and find him . . .

His leg needs rest.

Jésus! It's not your farm they'll burn down.

You can lie in the hayloft, and if they come back you can be working on top of the hay, the Cocadrille said.

And if he's asleep?

I'll stay with him.

Stay with him! In God's name! We have this hay to get in.

The Aunt is right, said the peasant from the Dranse, you should listen to her.

Half the hayloft was empty; in the other half the new hay was stacked almost as high as the roof beams. When she shut the door it was like twilight. She told the wounded man, who was young enough to be her son, on no account to hide in the hay, for the previous year a maquisard hiding in another farm had buried himself in the hay and the Italian soldiers had searched the loft, sticking in pitchforks. One of the prongs had wounded him in the neck. He dared not cry out. The Italian soldiers dawdled in the barn, joking with the peasant's wife. And the wounded man bled to death in the blood-red hay.

They know they are defeated now. Couldn't you see it in the officer's eyes? said the young man.

The Cocadrille shrugged her shoulders.

What will you do when the war stops?

I will continue my studies, he said.

And one day become a judge like your father?

No, it is another kind of justice that I believe in, a popular justice, a justice for peasants like you and for workers, a justice which gives factories to those who work in them, and the land to those who cultivate it. As he said this, he smiled shyly, as if confessing something intimate.

Is your father rich? she asked.

Fairly.

Won't you inherit some of his money?

All of it when he dies.

There's the difference between us.

She had a habit of kicking off one sabot and rubbing the bare foot against her other leg.

I shall use that money to start a paper. By then we shall have a free press. A free press is a prerequisite for the full mobilisation of the masses.

Are your feet hot too? she asked.

The hay is dusty, he said. He gravely gave everything he said equal thought.

Meanwhile you are in danger, she commented.

Not more than you.

That is true, today we are equal.

Do your brothers think like you?

I don't think.

I didn't trust them, he said.

They are as straight as a goat's hind leg. You must rest now. Later I will dress your wound again. What is your first name?

They call me Saint-Just.

I have never heard that name. Rest now, Saint-Just.

He slept without stirring. In the evening whilst the others were eating, she took him bread and a plate of soup.

I feel stronger, he announced.

I can dress your wound again.

No, just sit beside me.

When she sat beside him, he laid his head in her lap and she combed his hair with her fingers.

You have very gentle hands, he said for the second time.

It's like raking hay, she said laughing.

She broke off the story there. I do not know whether they made love. Perhaps it is only my own memories which make me ask the question. Yet there was something in the way the Coca- drille recounted her meetings with men which always left you speculating.

The two maquisards departed next day. Within forty-eight hours the village heard that a group of maquisards had been sur- prised in their camp by the Milice, taken prisoner, transported to A . . . and shot in a field there. There were six in the group and they included the peasant from the Dranse and Saint-Just. It was said that the Milice could never have found the camp, unless they had been tipped off by an informer.

The Cocadrille shrieked when she heard the news. At supper that night she was still crying with bloodshot eyes.

In God's name stop it, woman! Henri's wife exclaimed. In any case a woman of your age should be ashamed!

Those who sleep with dogs, wake up with fleas, said Edmond.

That's good! shouted Henri. That's good! Those who sleep with dogs, wake up with fleas!

She never forgave the insult. She began, as she had done when she was a child, to disappear. Without telling her brothers, she would be absent for a whole day, sometimes two days and a night. It became impossible to confide any regular job to her. She grad- ually withdrew her labour, as job after job appeared to her shame- ful. Not shameful in itself, but shameful for her to perform for two men whom she could not forgive.

Soon she was no longer on speaking terms with anybody in the house. She slept in the stable. She ate by herself. To save the bother of eating more than once a day, she rolled herself cigarettes. Her brothers were in constant dread that deliberately or acciden- tally she would set fire to the farm. They threatened to beat her if they found her smoking in the stable. In revenge she put an unlit cigarette in her mouth whenever she saw one of them approaching.

It was Henri who first spoke in the village of the Cocadrille's stealing. She stole, he said, eggs from his wife's chicken house. Since she doesn't work, he added, she has no right to them, and she sells them for money.

Some believed him and sympathised; others argued that she was, after all, his sister and he owed her her share of the inheritance. Gradually it became apparent that she was stealing from other gardens. A few lettuces, some plums, a marrow or two. Nobody, except Henri and Edmond, took these small thefts very seriously. They were humiliated by them.

The end came with the fire. The Cabrol grenier burnt down one autumn morning. The two brothers accused the Cocadrille of having deliberately set light to it.

They went to see the Mayor and they told him that they could no longer take responsibility for the actions of their sister, whose unleashed madness was Stealing and Arson. The Mayor was reluctant to refer the matter to any outside authority. It was his wife who thought of the solution which he finally proposed to Henri and Edmond. They accepted it enthusiastically. And with this proposal the first life of the Cocadrille came to an end.

The Second Life of
Lucie Cabrol

HOW LONG DISTANCES seem to a peasant may depend on how he cultivates his land. If he grows melons between cherry trees, five hundred metres is a considerable distance. If he grazes cows on a mountain pasture, five kilometres is not far. To the Cocadrille, who could cultivate nothing, because she now had no land, twenty kilometres became a short distance. She walked fast. When she was an old woman, people still commented on how quickly she disappeared. One moment they saw her on a path: the next moment hillside and skyline were empty. She usually carried a sack and, sometimes, tied across her back, a large blue umbrella.

One September morning in 1967 she set out early. The place she was making for was a high forested plateau, about eight kilometres away from where she now lived. When a pine tree falls in that forest, struck by lightning, or its roots are torn out of the earth by a gale, it lies where it fell until its wood turns grey, stifled by snow in winter and burnt by the sun in summer. There are no paths there. You can see on the fallen tree trunks hundreds of systematically dismantled pine-cones, which the squirrels have eaten, undisturbed since the thaw in the spring. Everywhere, climbing over roots and boulders, wild raspberries grow.

The canes were taller than she. As she picked them she crooned. This was to frighten the snakes. With her left hand she bent the canes back so that their under-sides, clustered with fruit, were uppermost: then, between the finger and thumb of her right hand she picked, going from cluster to cluster, until she was so far stretched over the cane that she risked falling forward on to her face. Any fruit that failed to come away easily from their white cores she left. Those she picked she put in the palm of her left hand. The berries were warm and granular like nipples. She held them in her calloused dirt-lined palm without squashing them. When she could hold no more she turned round and emptied the handful into a frail made of thin wood. As she moved forward through the forest, she left behind her thousands of white cores from which she had taken the fruit.

I was watching her. I had climbed up to the forest the same morning to look for bolets which grow along its upper edge, where the pines stop. To my surprise I saw a very small old woman in black among the trees. Since my return I had only heard about the Cocadrille from others.

After I arrived in Buenos Aires I seldom gave her a thought. If she came to mind at all, I congratulated myself on my luck in escaping her guile. I remained convinced that she had tried to trap me into marriage. Fortunately she had failed—probably because she was sterile. Contrary to what one might expect, as time passed, I thought of her more often. I took for granted my luck in not having become entangled with her. And in the hot airless nights of the city, not far from one of the vilest shanty towns, I used to picture to myself an alpine summer. One of the things I recalled was the long grass beneath the stars beside the Cabrol chalet. And then even her plotting seemed to me to belong to a life that was carefree and innocent.

Among the trees in the forest, she straightened her back from time to time and ate some of the fruit. I hid so she would not see me. I wanted to watch her unawares.

After twenty-five years in the Argentine, I went north to Montreal where, for a while, I was rich. I had my own bar there. Sometimes I would tell my story about the goats in the moonlight and the Cocadrille. Once a client asked me: Was this woman a dwarf? And I had to explain. No, she was not a dwarf, she was tiny, she was underdeveloped, she was ignorant, she was like a dwarf, but she wasn't. If she was physically like a dwarf, the client reasoned, she surely was a dwarf. No, I said.

When I next looked towards the forest, she had disappeared. Not a branch moved. The red cones hung motionless, they were especially, obscenely red that year. I have never seen them so red—

as red as the arseholes of baboons. There was no sign of her. I told myself I had imagined seeing her. Yet, when I walked over to where I thought she had been, the raspberry canes were stripped and you could see everywhere the white cores of the fruit she had taken.

A few days previously I had overheard some children coming out of school talking about her.

It makes you frightened just to meet her on the road.

Why does she live up there, so far away, next to the precipice?

Mother says she catches marmots and skins them.

My father says she has a fortune hidden up there.

Why doesn't she have a dog at least to keep her company?

Witches don't have dogs, they have cats.

If she looks at you, you have to open your mouth—have you noticed that—you can't keep it shut!

I was walking with my head down looking for mushrooms. With age I have become somewhat deaf. Something made me look to the side. The woman in the black dress, not more than ten metres away, was squatting at the foot of a tree, holding her dress up over her scratched knees.

The passer-by, she cawed, should always raise his hat to the one who is shitting!

I took off my beret and she cawed with laughter.

I think she didn't recognise me for when she got to her feet and took a few steps towards me, pulling down her skirt, she stopped and exclaimed.

It's Jean!

I nodded.

Do you recognise me?

You're the Cocadrille.

No! she said and her laughter stopped dead.

Why are you following me? she asked.

I came up here to look for bolets.

You found some?

What?

Did you find some? she insisted.

I opened my haversack. Her hair was white, the lines to the

corners of her mouth were very deep, and down the sides of her face I could see tracks of sweat. Around her lips were spots and traces of dark red from the fruit she had eaten. This, with her lined face and white hair, gave her the macabre air of a prematurely aged child. Or of an old person become childish.

Give them to me. Her eyes were fixed on the bolets I had found.

What for?

They are mine! she claimed.

She believed that whatever grew and had not been planted by man, within a radius of ten kilometres of where she lived, was incontestably hers.

I closed my haversack. She shook her head and turned away, cursing quietly to herself.

So you've come back, she said after a minute.

Yes, I've come back.

You were away too long. She stared at me with the intense gaze of her blue eyes, which were no more like flowers but like a stone called kyanite.

I remembered the way up here, I said.

You came up here to spy on me.

Spy?

Spy on me!

Why should I want to spy on you?

Give me the bolets then.

No.

Why did I refuse? I had found the mushrooms, therefore they were mine. It was an elementary point of justice. Yet I knew that justice had little to do with my life or hers. I refused out of habit.

She took an empty frail from her sack and began picking. I wondered how she arranged the frails in her sack when they were full so that the fruit would not be damaged.

Whilst you were away, everything changed, she said to me over her shoulder.

A lot must have changed when you left the farm.

I didn't leave it. They disinherited me.

She moved on, following the fruit, away from me. Soon she

appeared to forget that I was there. She bent back a stem on which the berries must have been especially closely clustered.

Thank you, little sow, she cawed. Thank you!

Did you marry out there? she shouted.

Yes.

I forced my way through the brambles so as to hear her better. She wore boots with no stockings and her scratched legs were as lean as the forelegs of a cow.

Why did you come back alone then?

My wife died.

You're a widower.

I am a widower.

Do you have children?

Two sons. They are both working in the United States.

Money can change everything, she said. She held up her left hand, full of raspberries, pretending that it was full of coins. He who hasn't got money is like a wolf without teeth. She looked around at the whole forest as if it were the world. And for he who has money, money can do anything. Money can eat and dance. Money can make the dirty clean, the despised respected. Money can even make the dwarf big.

Her using the word *dwarf* shocked me.

I have two million! she cawed.

I hope you keep them in a bank.

Fuck off! she swore. Fuck off and get away!

She pointed as if pointing at a door and ordering me out of a room rather than a forest. Everyone in the village said that she was fearless. I don't think this was true. What she counted on was inspiring fear in others. She knew that people were frightened of her. Now she was angry because she had told me about her savings; she had probably intended to keep this a secret. If I went obediently she might assume that I was not interested. If I insisted upon staying it would be tantamount to admitting my curiosity. So I left.

It is said that large mushrooms are large from the moment they first appear. One morning there is nothing, and the next morning the mushroom is there as large as it will ever be. A small mushroom is not a young large one. It will stay small, as the Cocadrille stayed small.

Occasionally, as I went on looking for my mushrooms, I saw her faded blue sunshade in the distance. Its blue was like the colour of her eyes. They had lost none of their colour with age. They had simply become dry, like stone.

Towards midday I found the largest bolet I have ever seen. I looked at it for several minutes before I saw it. Then suddenly it stood out from its surroundings of fern, moss, dead wood, grey pine needles and earth—exactly as if it had grown from nothing before my eyes. It was thirty centimetres in diameter and thick like a round loaf of bread. Sometimes I dream of finding mushrooms and even in my dream I say to myself: Don't pick them straight away, admire them first. This one weighed two kilos and was still fresh.

I walked to another part of the forest where the pines are not spruce but larches, and where the earth is covered with a carpet of turf as soft as an animal's stomach. There I planned to eat my lunch and afterwards, as has become my habit, to sleep a little. I put my beret over my face to keep the sun out of my eyes. And as I lay there, before I fell asleep, I thought, I must look like an old man who never left his country. This thought along with the mushrooms I had found, the little wine I had drunk, the softness of the turf, was a consolation. I sat up to look once more at the giant bolet in my haversack. It too was a confirmation that I had come home.

God in heaven!

If she hadn't sworn, she wouldn't have woken me. A platoon could march on the turf there without making a sound. She was holding the bolet which was as large as a loaf and staring at it. The strap of my haversack was already over her shoulder. She saw me sit up. This in no way deterred her. With her exaggeratedly long strides she was making off towards the other part of the forest. Why didn't I protest? To lose all the mushrooms I had gathered during the morning, to lose the largest bolet I had ever seen, and to lose a haversack into the bargain was a shouting matter. I could have run after her, picked her up and shaken her. I stayed there on the ground. All the stories I had heard about her were true. She was shameless. She was a thief. I had no doubt she would sell my mushrooms. Why had she not asked me for them once more? I might have given her some. The idea came to me that this time, and this time only, I would let her have what she had taken.

I need my haversack, I shouted.

You know where I live!

She bawled this as if it were a complete justification of what she had done.

A few days later I went to retrieve my haversack. Half an hour's walk along the road which climbs east out of the village brings you to a stone column on top of which is a small statue of the Madonna. She stands there arms relaxed, palms of her hands facing the road as if waiting to welcome the traveller. Either side of the Madonna are railings because, behind her, there is a sheer drop to the gravel of the river Jalent, sixty, seventy metres below.

Around the next bend of the road is the house in which the Cocadrille lived her second life. Beside the house there is a rock, as tall as the roof, with an ash tree growing on top of it. You have the impression that the house is jutting out into the road, edging away from the precipice behind its back. It was originally built before the First World War for a roadmender. He lodged there with his horse during the few weeks of the year when he was working on that isolated stretch of the pass. With the advent of lorries, the house no longer served any purpose and so was locked up and the key kept in the Mayor's office. The Mayor's wife's proposal had been that the Cocadrille should live in the road-mender's house rent-free. There, she would be far enough away from the village to cause trouble to nobody, and the law would not have to be invoked against her.

If you approach the roadmender's house from the opposite di-rection, you don't see it until you are beside it, for it is completely hidden by the rock with the tree on top of it. The rock is like a second house that has been filled with stone. From the direction I was approaching I could see a window, which had no curtains, in the house which was lived in.

I knocked on the door.

Who is it?

Jean.

You're too late.

It's not half past eight.

The door opened a fraction.

What do you want?

I have come to fetch my haversack.

At this hour!

I won't come in.

Now she opened the door fully.

I'll pay you a coffee.

The room was full of sacks and cardboard boxes, there were two piles of wood and so far as I could see, only one chair at a table, on which there was a pile of old newspapers, a heap of hazel-nuts and some knitting. The blue umbrella stood in a corner. The ceiling was smoked dark brown like the hide of a ham. The room was the size of a small lorry.

She continued doing what she must have been doing before I knocked. She gathered the hazel-nuts into a basket and hung them on a pair of scales, the traditional kind made of iron, which, on the banknotes of some countries, the figure of Justice holds up in front of her bosom.

Shit and shit! she grumbled. I can't see in this light.

I put on my glasses and looked over her shoulder to read the markings on the iron bar.

Six kilos, three hundred, I said.

She smelt of the floor of a forest into which the sun never penetrates, she smelt of boar.

After they were weighed she put the nuts into a cardboard box.

I haven't had a visit for three years. I had to strain my ears to hear her. She was speaking as if to herself. The last visitor I had was Monsieur le Curé in July 1964. They put me here to get me out of the way. Why don't you take your glasses off? They make you look like a curé.

If you can't read, you should wear glasses yourself.

Read! she cawed. Read!

From the pocket of her apron she took out a packet of tobacco and slowly rolled herself a cigarette. On the stove she moved a saucepan of milk to get a light from the burning wood.

If I turn my back you spill over, she said to the milk.

A cock came through the door from the adjoining stable. It stood there, one claw poised in the air.

Sit on the chair! she said. It was the last curé, not this one. He was always in bad health. He'd climbed up here on foot on his way somewhere. I offered to pay him a glass of water. Ah, he said, as soon as he came in: You are a child of the earth, Lucie. Without land, I said. You must not harbour resentment, he told me, you have things to be grateful for. I knew what he meant. Like this house you mean—everybody whispers that I don't pay rent for it and what a shack it is! It was built for one man and a horse—she lifted the milk off the fire—and when the horse died it wasn't lived in any more. I'm the only woman who ever slept in this house. I asked the curé to name one other woman in the village who would live here alone. None of them is a child of the earth, he repeated. I will show you one day what I am, I said, I'm going to surprise you all! It is dangerous—I remember how solemn his voice was—to hope too much; you cannot please the world and there is no reason to envy it. She shooed the cock away into the stable. Father, I said, I believe in happiness! And do you know what happened then? His face went white and he grasped my arm. Lucie, is there a little more water? he whispered. I gave him some *gnôle* and he drank it like water. He started to speak as if he were reading the Bible in church. It is written, sadness has killed many, and there is no profit in it. You are right, my daughter, to believe in happiness. Lie down, Father, I told him, and rest a moment. Where? he asked, I see no bed. I got him to the table. He lay down, closed his eyes and smiled. The angels, he murmured, who descended and ascended on Jacob's ladder, they had wings, yet they did not fly and they trod the gradual rungs of the ladder. I held the glass for him and undid the buttons where his clothes were too tight. He never opened his eyes. He will be ashamed when he wakes up, I said. He heard me say this because he spoke: I'm ashamed now but I feel better. Slowly, Father, I said, let your strength come back slowly. That was the last visitor I had. She poured out some coffee.

Haven't Henri or Edmond ever visited you?

It was then that she told me the story of her brothers and the maquisards. She told it squatting on a sack beside the stove. The kitchen grew darker and darker. I could see nothing except the orange of the fire in the stove and her white hair which gave off a glimmer of light. Outside there was a hard moon. They are traitors, she added, when she had finished the story.

Traitors?

It was they who informed the Milice.

Have you any proof?

I don't need proof. I know them too well.

Why should they have done that? The war was nearly over. Everyone saw the Germans were losing.

What kind of patriot were you? she hissed. A thousand kilometres away.

Ten thousand, I said.

She spat and rubbed the spittle with her foot on the floorboards.

The only time my brothers came here was when they brought my furniture. They made excuses all day saying they had to finish planting the potatoes. It was in April 1949. Only after they had eaten their soup did they load the cart. Then we set out under cover of darkness. Do you know why? In the daylight they were ashamed to be seen moving their sister out. When we arrived here, it was as dark as it is now. My own brothers, fed on the same mother's milk, sperm of the same father's sperm, left me here in the dark one night. I didn't even have a lamp. Each month they were meant to pay me. Pay my arse! I saw the last of them that same night through the window there.

I watched the cart go, she continued, and when I knew it was far away, I followed it. I went as far as the Madonna. She walked to the dark window in the room and stood looking out through the glass.

There was a long white cloud in the shape of a fish, she went on, I have never seen it again. Where the fish's eye should have been was the moon. I waited there at the foot of the Madonna's column and I spoke to Maman and Papa. You should have known your sons better, I told them. You always thought of them as they were when they were in the cradle. Shit! You didn't know where their evil came from, did you? You died, Papa, didn't you, not knowing that to make a child you need a woman, a man and the Devil. That's why it's so tempting! I saw what Papa was doing at that very moment when I was standing at the Madonna's feet. He was rutting into Maman. And Maman was pulling him down! When you were alive, you didn't do it enough, did you, you were always too tired and your back felt too broken. Go on. I give you my blessing. Go on, I told them. You have nothing left here. Your sons will give nothing back to you. If you speak out loud, they won't listen. If you stopped and saw me, you'd suffer. I'm not going to let you suffer, Papa, I'm not going to let you suffer, Maman, because I'm going to survive. You carcasses with your backs to everything! I'm not going to let you suffer. I swear it. I'm going to survive.

In the darkness the room smelt of sacks and earth. A car came up the road and its headlights shone straight through the window at which she stood, lighting up the entire room. In this light, the room looked more than ever like a store shed. In the corner, on the far side of the stove, was a ladder and above it an open trapdoor. When the car had passed, the darkness by contrast was total. The noise of the engine died away. In the silence and darkness, the two of us could as well have been in our coffins.

Do you want to eat some soup with me?

I have a bottle of wine.

So you thought you'd stay!

No, I bought it for myself at home.

After forty years' absence, what have you got to show? One litre of wine!

A little more.

What?

Enough to live on till I move to the Boulevard of the Laid Out.

So you've come back to die.

We're not young any more.

I'm not ready to die yet, she proclaimed.

Death doesn't ask if you are ready.

Are you going to live well? she asked.

I'm not rich. I didn't make the fortune I dreamt of. I was unlucky. Do you always sit in the dark?

What did you find in South America—electricity? I go to bed when I can't see. You're going to keep your mother's house in the village?

I bought it from my brothers.

When did you do that?

This interrogation, during which we were both invisible to the other, reminded me of kneeling before the confession box. I sent them money when I had it.

She must have read my thoughts, for the next question she asked was: Were you faithful to your wife?

What a man does with his own skin, I said, is his own business.

For twenty years I haven't spoken to anyone after nightfall except my chickens and the goat, when I still had one.

Give me my haversack and I'll be going.

No, wait! I'll light the lamp.

She struck a match and made her way over to the cupboard, in which she found a candle.

Are you hot now? she asked the soup, lifting the lid of the saucepan with as much caution as she had first opened the door to me. I can't grow a single potato for you, they've taken every one. Can you lift the lamp down? Otherwise I have to stand on a chair.

The lamp was on the mantelpiece. I lit it. She climbed up the ladder to the loft and came down with a second chair. From the nail in the wall behind the stove she took a pewter ladle and rubbed it against the side of her black dress.

At last we sat down on either side of the table. The soup was steaming in the plates. It must have been past midnight.

So you have brought nothing back with you! She looked into my face.

Not a great fortune.

That's obvious.

She held out her glass for me to fill with wine.

I swore to survive and become rich, and rich I've become, she said. There's no man on earth who has the right to a single glass of vin blanc paid for out of my money! From now on I'm going to drink wine in the evenings.

What time do you get up in the mornings? I asked. I must be going.

In time to milk.

You have no cows.

I get up in time to milk. Every morning for the twenty years since I've been here.

At five?

She nodded.

You have an alarm clock?

In here. She pointed at her white hair.

And tomorrow? I asked.

Tonight is an exception, she said, holding out her glass for me to refill. Tonight I'm going to tell you about the twenty years.

What have they to do with me?

You have come back a pauper yet at least you have seen the world.

When she swore at the feet of the Madonna to survive, she had no clear idea of how to become rich. She knew less than I did when I took the boat to Buenos Aires. All she knew was that she could not become rich in the village.

I have renamed the village, she said. I have renamed it *Chez Cocadrille*! She shook with laughter and licked her colourless lips with her pink tongue.

Fifty kilometres away, just over the frontier, was the city of B . . . . Marius à Brine had spoken of its wealth, just as his father had done. Marius also said that those who lived in B . . . gave nothing away; they were so mean that they melted the snow to give what was left as alms to the poor! The Cocadrille concluded as she watched her two lost parents embracing that the place where money truly existed was B. . . . Such money as reached the village was vagrant money. She had to go to its home, where money bred.

What could she take to sell in B . . . ? It was the moment for killing kids and she had no goats. It was the time when last summer's cheeses were ready to eat, and she had no cows. It was the laying season for chickens and she had not yet built her chicken-run. The solution, obvious as it was, did not come to her immediately. She walked back along the moonlit road from the Madonna's column.

I slept down here the first night, she said. It took me a year to move up to the loft. I missed the animals in the stable, and the idea of sleeping half-way up the sky, in the cold, didn't appeal to me. I prefer to sleep on the ground, don't you?

For a while I lived on the eighteenth storey.

What did it bring you?

She rubbed index finger against thumb in the banknote gesture which signifies money. Then she touched the back of my hand with her fingers.

During the first night in the roadmender's house, she dreamt of the Madonna. The Madonna spoke to her in her dream and told her that everything which people go out to pick, she must pick first and take to the city. This is why the Madonna's hands were open and pointing to the grass on the verge of the road.

Next day she took the path up to the highest fields of the village. The altitude there is nine hundred metres, and the grass was only just beginning to grow. She picked dandelions for salad, their leaves still very small, their stalks white. She didn't come down until she had picked two kilos. Then she set out for the fields and orchards five hundred metres below, and there, where the dandelions were already flowering and the grass as high as her shins, she hunted for morels. Her fingers led her to them, under the pear trees, among nettles, between the stones of walls.

I still know where a mushroom is waiting, like a bitch on heat for a dog.

By the end of the day she had filled a basket.

At dusk she went out once again to collect violets and primroses at the edge of the forest. The violets she arranged in tiny bouquets with a damp cloth around them, and the primroses she cut out of the earth with their roots and soil attached. When it was fully night, she walked along the road to the Madonna's column and, in the grass at its base, she planted some of the primroses.

A train went to the frontier town which adjoins B. . . . There was even a song about this train which La Mélanie used to sing. The train in the song left the town at noon, and travelled so slowly and stopped so often by the river, the smoke from the engine going straight up into the sky, that it never reached the village till it was dark, a fact which delighted lovers because they could caress each other undisturbed in the warm upholstered carriages. La Mélanie used to mime their embraces whilst she sang. The Cocadrille took this train. It was going in the opposite direction to the train in the song and went much faster. The journey lasted less than two hours. What frightened her was its smoothness. She was used to lurches and bumps against which, without thinking, she tensed herself so as not to be bruised against the wood of the cart drawn by the horse. The smoothness of the train made her feel sick: it was as if the earth no longer existed.

When the train arrived at the end of the line, she followed everyone out of the station. She saw no one she knew to ask where the frontier was. She resolved to walk in the same direction as most of the men. It was still early in the morning and she knew that many men went to work for the day in B. . . .

At the frontier the douanier asked her whether she had anything to declare. She looked blank. What have you got with you? he asked. Some morels, she said. I'll sell them to you, if you offer me a good price!

After two hours' searching, she found the market. She walked through it to see whether others were selling the same goods as she had brought. There were no other violets, and she thought she had misread the price of the dandelion leaves. They cost two hundred for a hundred grams. Two thousand a kilo! She understood better the wealth of the city of B. . . . The morels were selling at five thousand a kilo! She chose a corner in the shade, put her baskets down either side of her feet and waited for customers to come and buy. She stood waiting all morning. At midday she saw all the other traders packing up their stalls. She had sold nothing. She had not opened her mouth.

On her way back to the frontier she went into a café to ask for a glass of water. Nowhere in the streets had she seen a pump or a fountain. The proprietor peered into her basket of morels. He picked one up without a word, turned it in his fingers.

I'll give you a thousand for the basketful.

There are two kilo there. You can weigh them.

I don't need to.

They're selling for five thousand a kilo in the market, she said, scandalised.

He shrugged his shoulders and turned away. She stared at him, her chin level with the top of his zinc bar. Looking over his shoulder, he opened his silent mouth and guffawed with laughter.

How much do you weigh yourself! he asked. You could throw yourself in for good measure! I'll give you twelve hundred.

She saw that she had to accept the price, it was her last chance.

It took her a year to find her way about B. . . . In Buenos Aires I saw peasants newly arrived in the city, and all of them had the same air of confusion and extreme timidity. Many of them never got over it. I and the Cocadrille did. Of the two of us, she was the quicker. At home, in the village, it is you who do everything, and the way you do it gives you a certain authority. There are accidents and many things are beyond your control, but it is you who have to deal with the consequences even of these. When you arrive in the city, where so much is happening and so much is being done and shifted, you realise with astonishment that nothing is in your control. It is like being a bee against a window pane. You see the events, the colours, the lights, yet something, which you can't see, separates you. With the peasant it is the forced suspension of his habit of handling and doing. That's why his hands dangle out of his cuffs so stupidly.

Month by month the Cocadrille learnt where she could sell each item in the city, each item which, according to the season, she scavenged from the mountains: wild cherries, lilies of the valley, snails, mushrooms, blueberries, raspberries, wild strawberries, blackberries, *trolles*, juniper berries, cumin, wild rhododendra, mistletoe.

You have to understand that everything you watch in the city is as unimportant as a game. Everything which impresses you about the city is an illusion. It is not easy. To be impressed and unimpressed at the same time! What really happens in a city is hidden. If you want to achieve anything it must be arranged in secret.

She went to cafés, never missing a wink or a nod, never failing to remember a quickly suggested address. She bought a map of the city and on it she marked, with the flowing capital letters which André Masson taught us all, the addresses of her customers.

You'd have to pay to see that map! she cawed.

I poured out the last of the wine.

Do you remember where the cumin grows on the path to the alpage? I bring down a pailler full on my back and I let it dry there in the stable. I put newspapers underneath for the seeds to fall on to. I can sell a hundred grams of cumin seed for one thousand, five hundred!

As she named the price, she tapped with all the fingers of one hand on the edge of the table, and the spoon rattled in her plate. She discovered that there was no need to pay for a ticket to travel to B. . . . She could stop lorries and cars on the road and they would take her. She went to the city twice a week. All the other days of the year, when there wasn't snow, she scavenged from dawn to dusk.

Drivers came to know me. She touched the back of my hand again. Sometimes they tried to take liberties but they never tried twice.

Réné, the electrician, picked her up one day.

As far as the frontier? she asked.

Réné nodded and she got in the back. He saw her in the driving mirror. It was a new car he had just bought and she sat in the very centre of the shining back seat, bolt upright with her sack on the floor. Réné nudged the apprentice sitting beside him.

Have you heard the story of the he-goat who went mad?

No.

He belonged to a farm where, years before, a cock laid an egg. How's that?

The peasant's wife was certain because one morning she went into the chicken house and there was the cock on one of the hens' boxes, making laying noises. She shooed him off and there was an egg! Saying nothing to her husband, she took the egg and buried it in the dung heap. Four weeks later . . .

He was interrupted by the noise of something crackling. He turned around. The Cocadrille was lying back with her legs and boots in the air. On the seat beside her, several egg yolks were running down the upholstery. The scraps of newspaper from which she had unwrapped the eggs were still on her lap.

Finish your story, she said. What did the Cocadrille do to the billy-goat?

Réné drove on in silence. When the douanier at the frontier asked whether they had anything to declare, the Cocadrille leant forward and said:

The two men here have a dozen broken eggs to declare.

Réné shook his head and winked at the douanier.

You can count them there on the floor, she insisted, twelve, and they haven't paid me for them yet. A car like this, and they pretend they can't pay an old woman for a dozen eggs!

How did they break? asked the douanier, laughing.

A billy-goat rolled on them . . . she explained, and, without a thank-you or a good-bye, the Cocadrille got down from the car and followed the tram-lines.

She learnt that money did not have the same value on both sides of the frontier. For everything bought, there was a cheap side and an expensive side. She learnt that it was foolish to bring money back; less foolish to bring back what she could sell expensively on her side.

We are surrounded by natural frontiers: snow, mountains, rock walls, rivers, ravines. For centuries we have also lived near an invisible political frontier. Where exactly it runs, changes according to the force of foreign governments and armies. This frontier divides the rich from the poor, and it is the easiest of all to cross.

The threat of being flogged, of exile, of execution, of being sent to the galleys, has never deterred men or women from crossing it and smuggling. Many smuggled alone; some formed bands like small armies. The names of the leaders of these bands she knew by heart: Le Grand Joseph, Le Dragon, La Danse à l'Ombre, the great Louis Mandrin who was executed at V. . . .

What have you got to declare today, Grandma?

Down to there, nothing, she pointed to the pit of her stomach, underneath there is a present for any young man who wants it!

Besides the map which she would not show me, she kept an almanac. In it, each year, she wrote down the date of the month when a crop in a given place was ready for picking. Five days a week, for she was also out scavenging on Sundays, she combed the countryside. Like a crow, she noticed everything.

She knew not only paths but countless clearings, assemblies of rocks, streams, fallen trees, protected hollows, fissures, crests, slopes. It was only for the city of B . . . that she needed a map. She knew exactly where to crawl along the border of the forest to find wild strawberries. She knew under which pine trees the cyclamen grow, the tiny cyclamen which are called *pain de porceau* because wild boar eat their roots. She knew on which distant precipitous slope the first rhododendra flower. She knew by which walls whole settlements of snails come out of hiding. She knew where the yellow gentians with the largest roots grow on the mountainside where the soil is least rocky so that digging them is a little easier. She worked and scavenged alone.

I talk to my shadow when the sun is out, and together we calculate the price our loot is likely to fetch. We have become experts, the two of us. And we commiserate together—about the weight of the sack, about the thorns in our hands, about how long we work. Sometimes, like you, we sleep at midday.

Abruptly she pushed back her chair, and went over to the cupboard.

Do you still drink gnôle?

It's very late, I complained.

The contempt of her laughter filled the room. She poured from the bottle into the glasses.

I sell a bottle of this for nine thousand!

It was the first gentian which I had tasted since my return. It has a very strong taste. The gentian roots taste of the earth and the earth tastes of the mountain.

She knew where every accessible wild cherry tree was. She carried a small ladder with her, no taller than herself, and this enabled her to get up into the tree. When she was well placed, her back against a branch, her boots on another, surrounded by cherries, and the basket hung from its hook at the right level, she could pick without looking. She could stand in the tree with her eyes shut like an owl, and her fingers would find the stalks, instantly move down them and break them off at the hode four or five at a time. With her eyes half shut she scarcely touched the fruit.

She sold her goods to restaurants, herbalist shops, florists, hotel manageresses.

I'll give you three thousand for the silver thistles, said the manageress, are you deaf, can you hear me? She held out a five-thousand note.

I have no change, said the Cocadrille.

If you never have change, how do you get here every week? demanded the manageress angrily.

By private car!

The manageress was forced to go and change the note. May she rot! added the Cocadrille.

One afternoon there was a cloudburst and she found herself propelled into a crowd of women, who surged through the glass doors of a department store and came to a stop before a glass counter where young women were selling stockings and lace underwear. No sooner had she begun to marvel at the black lace, than she was again pushed from behind, and this time found herself surrounded by other women in a lift. When it went up, she crossed herself and whispered:

Emile, if only you could see me now!

The lift operator, a man of her own age, dressed in a bandsman's uniform, said to her: Coffee, tea, chocolate, pâtisseries, Madame.

The lift doors slid back and the two carpeted ground levels once more coincided.

For the next ten years, every week, after she had sold her goods, she visited this upper floor tea-room. On her way to the tea-room she went to a tobacconist.

What can I do for you today, Madame?

Give me eight hundred Marlboro.

The tobacconist slipped the four large packets into a gold-coloured plastic bag. Carrying the gold-coloured bag, she entered the department store, crossed to the lift and waited for the liftman to address her: Coffee, tea, chocolate, pâtisseries, Madame?

On the fourth floor she went to the ladies' room. There she locked herself in the lavatory and pulled up her long black serge skirt. Underneath, at the level of her hips, she wore a cloth band. This bandoleer she had made out of one of La Mélanie's linen chemises. Its pockets were larger than the usual ones for cartridges. Before sewing them she had measured very carefully. Into the double line of pockets she fitted thirty-nine packets of Marlboro.

With these red-and-white packets of what she considered to be tasteless tobacco, she was able to double her income. American cigarettes sold for twice as much on her side of the frontier. After she had arranged her skirt and pulled down her loose cardigan she flushed the toilet and emerged, hat in hand. She arranged her hair in the mirror above the wash-basin.

She had the appearance of a pauper and at the same time she looked wilful. Such a combination in a city suggests madness.

The drinking of the chocolate she ordered in the tea-room was a ritual, and was accompanied by her smoking one or two cigarettes from the single packet she had kept out. She preferred the cigarettes she rolled herself. It was her sense of occasion which made her realise it would have been inappropriate to smoke them in such a setting.

This was the only moment of the week when she sat in company, although she spoke to no one except the waitress. Sitting there on one of the gilded wicker chairs, such as she had never seen until her second life began, sipping her chocolate with grated nutmeg sprinkled on its frothy cream, smoking a perfectly cylindrical cigarette with a long filter-tip, checking from time to time with her stiffened fingers that her bandoleer was in place, she allowed herself to dream of the fulfillment of her plans. She studied the other customers, nearly all of whom were women out shopping. She noticed their hands, their made-up faces, their jewelry, their shoes with high heels. She had no wish to speak to them and she did not envy them, yet the sight of them gave her pleasure. They were a weekly proof of the extent of what money can do. Each month she saved at least half the money which she received for the cigarettes smuggled across the frontier. Never for an instant did she forget what the total of her savings amounted to. Every week this figure encouraged her. It was like a father. It got her out of bed when it was dark. When she set out, before the sun was up, on her walk of twenty kilometres, and her skirt was drenched by the dew which dripped down her legs into her socks, it reminded her that her dress might dry within an hour, if it didn't rain. When she was hungry, it told her not to complain, for she would eat later. When her back ached and her shoulders were sore and, coming down from the mountain, her knees were knotted and cracked with so much pain that it made her cry out, it reminded her how one day she would buy a new bed. When she talked with her shadow, it promised her that eventually they would move back into the village.

Whilst drinking her chocolate, the total of her savings—she always added on what she was about to receive that day—was as consoling as the music which came out of the loudspeakers high up near the decorated ceiling. Every week, every year, every decade, the amount increased.

When you have enough money, you can stand on your head stark naked!

She said this to a man, accompanied by a woman in a fur coat, who was waiting in the tobacconist's shop. The woman gave a little scream and the man, thinking that she was begging, dug into his trouser pocket for a small coin. The Cocadrille refused it. I have enough! she hissed at him. I have enough, she repeated to me across the table.

She sipped the gnôle and rolled herself another cigarette.

Soon it will be winter, she went on. Then I'm alone. And the snow forces me indoors. At Christmas I take mistletoe into B. . . . . I get a thousand for a good bunch. The rest of the time, I knit. I can do nothing else. I never learnt to spin like Maman. Anyway I have no sheep. I knit pullovers and ski caps for a shop in B. . . .

She gulped back the rest of the gnôle.

Next door to the wool shop there is an antique shop. There's a wooden cradle in the window at the moment. If I had mine, I would sell it. Once I went in there and asked the price of a milking stool. Can you guess how much it cost? If it costs that much, I told them, what would I cost? You could sell me piece by piece. You could ask one hundred thousand for a milking hand. You could ask fifty thousand for a milking arm. How much would you get, I asked them, for a real peasant woman's arsehole?

She drew on her cigarette.

All winter I knit. There's nothing here, day after day, except the two needles and me. When a car passes and doesn't stop— and they never stop—I think of shooting the driver. Why not?

Why do you tell me all this?

So that you should know what I'm saying.

Only the corners of the room were still dark. The flame in the lamp looked yellow and daylight was coming through the smeared, dusty windows. She took the lamp and I thought she was going to blow it out. Instead, she walked over to the chimney in the corner and held the lamp above her head.

Look! she ordered.

On the mantelpiece were several porcelain plates decorated with cherries and flowers, a statuette of a chamois standing on a rock with his head high in the air, and a white bust in porcelain of St François de Sales. Unlike everything else in the room, these objects were dusted, carefully arranged and shining.

Have you really saved two million? I asked.

She cocked her head on one side, like a blackbird when it is about to smash a snail against a stone.

I have been listening all night, I said. It's not as if you're hiding things from me!

She blew out the lamp, turned her back, and refused to utter another word.

Three days later, on returning home in the evening, I found a note rolled and put into the keyhole of my door. The Cocadrille must have passed through the village and found the door locked. The note, written in her large flowery hand, simply said: *If you want to hear more, I have more to tell you.* It was useless to visit her in the daytime for she might be anywhere in her vast territory, and so the following evening I took the road past the Madonna's column. When I turned the corner I saw to my surprise that there was already a light in the window of the roadmender's house. I knocked at the door.

Who is it?

Jean! I replied. Are you alone?

She undid the lock.

I wasn't expecting you.

I found your note.

What note?

The note you left in my door yesterday.

I wasn't in the village yesterday.

Who else could it have been?

Was it signed?

She demanded this mischievously as though she already knew or had guessed the answer.

No, it wasn't.

The store-room was unchanged, except that there were several bulging sacks in the corner under the ladder, and from their smell I knew they were full of gentian roots. Like roots, her own hands were caked with earth.

What have you done? she asked.

I was at the fair at La Roche.

I was by Le Forêt du Cercle.

In my head I tried to work out who, if not the Cocadrille, might have written the note. Whoever it was intended that I should believe it was written by the Cocadrille; it must have been written by somebody who knew that I had already visited her.

Why have you lit the lamp so early? I asked.

I was going to write.

Another note to me?

To somebody else.

It then occurred to me that, contrary to what she said, the Cocadrille was in the habit of receiving other visitors. And they were men, I felt sure of that. She used her jokes and stories as a bait to attract some company for a little while, to drink across the table—this is why she had commented on my bringing only one bottle of wine—and perhaps also out of a kind of malice, to make a little mischief with the men's wives. It was a previous visitor who must have written me the note.

Sit down, she said, I'll heat the soup.

I can't stay long.

You have so much to do!

She knelt down to blow into the fire and whisper into it: there is something I want to ask you. It was not clear whether she said this to the fire or to me.

She went out to the stable and I heard her washing her hands in a bucket of water.

What can I pay you? she asked when she came back.

A little red.

I carry everything up here on my back!

Is the white wine lighter?

She laughed at that, and glanced at me conspiratorially.

Wait! she ordered and climbed up the ladder.

The wood cracked as it caught fire in the stove. I went over to smell the soup—with age I have become greedy: not that I eat so much and not that, living alone, I cook special dishes for myself, it is simply that I think more about food, thoughts about food pester me like cats that have not been fed. I glanced up at the mantelpiece and the shining porcelain plates decorated with cherry-tree branches. I rubbed my finger on the shelf to check whether it had collected dust and I thought: How unpredictable the Cocadrille is!

Outside, the sun had set behind the Roc d'Enfer, I could tell because the distant rockface, where the cumin grows, had turned pink, the colour of pale coral. Usually it is as grey as wood ash.

I went out of the door onto the ledge. I could hear the Jalent below. They said in the village that the Cocadrille seldom washed her clothes; when a garment was rotten with dirt she simply threw it over the edge.

On the other side of the river were orchards and meadows with cows in them. They looked like a picture engraved on a wooden mould for butter. La Mélanie had had just such a mould showing a river at the bottom, two cows in the middle, and some apple trees in the distance. This was the mould the Cocadrille used in the alpage fifty years before.

I looked behind the chicken hutch, I walked right round the rock house with the tree on top of it, I went down the road as far as the corner, I surveyed the mountain above. Nobody was there. Whoever had written the note was going to play no practical joke tonight. I was slightly disappointed for had he come, we could have talked there on the road about the Cocadrille's stratagems. The air was turning cold, and I returned indoors.

The saucepan was steaming on the stove.

So you've seen the ledge I live on!

I looked up. She was standing half-way down the ladder. She had changed her clothes. She was wearing shoes, not sabots, some kind of silk stockings instead of woollen ones, a black heavy silk skirt, a white blouse, a jacket to match the skirt, and around her head and shoulders, a white tulle veil. She was dressed in the clothes in which women go to church to be married.

In God's name, what do you think you are doing! I shouted.

Her eyes were so intense that they forced you to share in their madness. I remember thinking: For the first time I understand why you are called the Cocadrille. Her eyes made both our long lives seem no more than a moment.

My poor Jean! You're shitting in your pants!

She came down the ladder, went over to the stove and dipped the ladle into the saucepan. Years before, her entry from the stable had so surprised me that I did not fully understand what she had done until the next day; it was only then that I realised how she must have sprinkled cow's milk on her breasts. This time I was more percipient. Clearly she had spent several evenings sewing the black silk costume. Even if, as was likely, she had inherited it from Mélanie, it would have been too large for the Cocadrille and would have required drastic alteration. She must have prepared this scene. It was part of a plan.

You certainly have a taste for theatre! I muttered.

There is no theatre in what I do.

Why do you dress up then?

The last time I undressed! She put her hands on her ribs as though to quieten the cackling of her own laughter.

We broke the bread and put it in the soup. Neither of us spoke and the silence was filled with the sound of her sucking from her spoon. She had fewer than half her teeth left. When she had finished, she pushed her plate away, got up, and came back with a bottle of gnôle. Of all the stories I had heard about her, none hinted that she was normally in the habit of drinking. Her shoes were brand new—as indeed they must have been, for nobody else's would have fitted her.

Do you dress up like this every time you invite a man up from the village?

Abruptly she drank back the *gnôle* in her glass. She drank it back like a chicken drinks, with a quick stupid toss of its head.

If I didn't have enough, she cried, I could go on for another ten years. I do have enough. I have scavenged for twenty years. I want to enjoy the rest of my life. I want to move back into the village. You have a house in the village and you haven't much else. I'm prepared to buy now a share of your house until I'm dead, and I will pay you straight away. The rest of my savings I'm keeping for myself. Does that interest you?

The house is too small.

I know.

The way you live—I looked deliberately round the kitchen— is not the way I could live. At my age I'm not going to change.

I can change. That's why I showed you the plates and the chamois.

I shook my head. Why don't you rent a whole house to yourself?

There are none. And it would be a waste of too much money.

Have you asked anyone else to take you in?

Only *you* know me! She whispered this as though we were not alone in the lonely house on the deserted road which led over the empty pass.

Was it you who wrote the note?

She nodded. I was writing to you again tonight.

What you really want, I shouted, is for me to marry you! That's what you have always wanted!

Yes, she said. In church, with this veil.

You are out of your mind.

There's no one to stop you this time. You are alone, she said.

God protect me.

I will pay you separately for the marriage, I'll give you a dowry.

You can't be that rich!

We can talk about money as soon as we agree in principle. She laid her hand on the back of mine.

I can't marry you.

Jean!

Again she said my name as she had said it forty years before and again it separated me, marked me out from all other men. In the mountains the past is never behind, it's always to the side. You come down from the forest at dusk and a dog is barking in a hamlet. A century ago in the same spot at the same time of day, a dog, when it heard a man coming down through the forest, was barking, and the interval between the two occasions is no more than a pause in the barking.

In the pause between her twice saying my name in the same way, I saw myself as the young boy I had once been, encouraged by Masson to believe that I was more than usually intelligent, I saw myself as a young man without prospects, because I was the youngest, but with great ambitions, my first departure for Paris which so impressed me as the centre, the capital of the globe, that I was determined to take one of the roads from l'Etoile across the world, the last good-byes to my family, my mother imploring me not to go all the time that I harnessed the horse and my father put my bag in the cart. It is the Land of the Dead, she said. The voyage by the boat on which each day I dreamt of how I would return to the village, honoured and rich with presents for my mother, I saw myself on the quayside where I did not understand a single word of what was being said, and the great boulevards and the obelisk, the grandeur of the packing plants which I tried to describe in a letter to my father, for whom the selling of one cow for meat was the subject of a month's discussion, the news of my father's death, the noise of the trains through the window of the room where I lodged for five years, Carmen's tantrums and her plans to open a bar of her own, her black hair the colour of the coal I shovelled, the epidemic in the shanty town, the land of straight railways so flat and going on forever; I saw myself in the train going south to Río Gallegos in Patagonia, sheep-shearing and a wind that, like my home-sickness, never stopped, I saw my wedding in Mar del Plata with all seventy-three members of Ursula's family, the birth of Gabriel six months later, the birth of Basil eighteen months afterwards and my fight with her family to christen him Basil, Ursula's dressmaking, her mother's debts, my friendship with Gilles and the pleasure of speaking my own language again, I saw Gilles' death, Ursula refusing to go to his funeral or to let the boys go, the flight to Montreal, the boys learning English which I could never speak, the news of my mother's death, the news of Ursula's death, the fire in the bar, the police investigations, I saw myself working as a night-watchman, my Sundays in the forest, the buying of my ticket home, I saw forty whole years compressed within the pause.

What separated me this time from all other men called Jean or Théophile or François was not desire, which is stronger than words, it was a sense of loss, an anguish deeper than any understanding. When she said my name the first time in the chalet in the alpage, she offered another life to the one I was about to live. Looking back I saw, now, the hope in the other life she offered and the hopelessness of the one I chose. Saying my name the second time, it was as if she had only paused a moment and then repeated the offer; yet the hope had gone. Our lives had dissolved it. I hated her. I would gladly have killed her. She made me see my life as wasted. She stood there and everything I saw—her wrinkled

cider-apple of a face, her stiff swollen hands which grabbed and
rooted the region like a boar's tusks, placed now with their palms
to her breast as if in supplication, the frail veil, the morsel of
cigarette-paper stuck to her lip, were all proof of the dissolution
of the offer. Yet I was forced—for the first and last time in this
life—to speak to her tenderly.

Give me time to think, Lucie!

My using her proper name caused her to smile and brought
tears to her eyes. For a moment their extraordinary sharpness was
clouded and the thousands of lines around them were doubled as
she screwed them up.

Come and tell me when you want to, Jean.

Before I gave her my considered answer, she was dead.

Her body was discovered by the postman who noticed that the
window onto the road was broken and swinging on its hinges.
The second morning he knocked and went in. She had been felled
with an axe. The blade had split her skull. The signs were that
she had put up a fight and had thrown a bottle through the window. Despite extensive searches, her fortune was never found.
The most likely explanation was that the murderer came to steal
her savings, had been surprised by her when he was leaving, and
had killed her. The axe was her own which he had taken from
the stable. The police cross-questioned almost everybody in the
village, including myself, yet they made no arrest and the murderer
was not identified.

She was buried a month before La Toussaint. There were fewer
than a hundred people at her funeral; her death was a kind of
disgrace for the village. She had been killed for her fortune and
only somebody from the village was likely to have known about
it. There were many flowers placed on her coffin, and the large
unsigned wreath I ordered was not immediately remarkable.

The Third Life
of Lucie Cabrol

ONE MORNING WHEN I was six my father said to me: When you let out the cows, keep Fougère behind, she's going to the abattoir today. I undid the chains of the other cows—I could just reach the locking links with my arms above my head—and the dog chased them out. Later I would take the cows to the slopes by the place which we called Nîmes. Left alone in the stable, Fougère looked anxiously around her, her ears full out like wings. By this afternoon, I said, you will be dead. She started to eat the hay in the manger. After pulling out several mouthfuls, each with a toss of her head, she looked around again and lowed. The other cows were already grazing outside. I could hear their bells. The sunlight coming through the holes in the planks of the stable walls made beams in the dust which I raised as I swept. My father unbuckled the wide leather collar Fougère was wearing. Attached to this collar was her bell which weighed five kilos. Before he turned away to hang the collar and the bell on the wall, he looked at the beast and said: My poor cuckoo, you'll never again go to Nîmes.

Whilst the funeral service was being performed inside the church, most of us men stood outside. This group of standing figures, solemn and still, always looks dwarfed by the mountains. We spoke in low voices, about the murder. Everyone was agreed that the police would never discover who the assassin was. Each said this as if he himself had a clear idea of the truth. She was fearless, they said, this had been the Cocadrille's trouble.

When the coffin came out of the church, the crowd followed it in procession through the cemetery. Nobody spoke now. The coffin was so small that it made you think of a child's funeral. It was in the cemetery that I first heard her voice. I had no difficulty in hearing what she said, although she was whispering.

Do you want me to say who it is? He's among you, he's here in the cemetery, the thief.

The murderer, I muttered.

It's the thief whom I cannot forgive!

Her voice made me frightened. I realised that the others could not hear it. My fear was that she would shout, and it would become obvious by my reactions that I could hear something.

What would you do if I shouted his name? she said, realising my thoughts.

They won't hear.

You will hear me, Jean, you can hear me if I say Jean, can't you.

Yes, I said, and made the sign of the cross over her coffin.

When once the coffin was passed, the procession shuffled forward more quickly.

It wasn't me.

You thought of killing me.

Outside the cemetery gate her brothers Edmond and Henri stood by the wall traditionally reserved after funerals for the closest of kin. If stones could feel, the stones there would be blood-red from the pain felt by many of those who have leant against them.

My brothers look solemn and hopeful, don't they? Solemn and hopeful!

The crowd dispersed and the men went to drink in the cafés. I declined several invitations and hurried away in order to lead her voice back home, where we would be unobserved.

In the house, the same house in which she had planned that we should live after we had married, I spoke to her. She did not reply. Indeed I had the impression she had not accompanied me. Perhaps she had gone to the cafés.

I awoke early next morning and went to look out of the window. The valley below was filled with opaque white mist; where it ended, little trails of transparent cloud blew off like steam into the sky. The valley was like a laundry, the endless laundry of the damned, steaming, soaping, billowing, working against the bath of the rockfaces in total silence. The lichen on the rocks were the voices of the damned.

Did you decide not to marry me?

I hadn't decided.

Then I'll leave you till you've made up your mind.

At La Toussaint the cemetery was full of flowers, and many people stood at the feet of the graves of their loved ones trying to listen to the dead. That night I heard her voice again. It was as close as if it were on the pillow beside mine.

I've learnt something, Jean. All over the world the dead drink at La Toussaint. Everyone drinks, no one refuses. Every year it is the same, they drink until they're drunk. They know that they have to visit the living. And so they get drunk!

On what?

On eau-de-vie! She spluttered with laughter and I felt her spit in my ear.

When she had got her breath back, she continued: And so they never know whether the living are as bone-headed as they seem, or whether the dead only have that impression because the dead are so drunk!

You sound drunk now.

Why did you think of killing me?

You know it wasn't I who stole your savings?

What did you want to kill me for?

You are drunk.

I tell you, nobody comes today if they are sober.

Has La Mélanie come?

She's making some coffee.

That will sober you up!

Not the black coffee of the dead won't. She cackled with laughter once more.

So you're drunk, every time you talk to me.

No, the dead forget the living, I haven't forgotten yet.

How long does it take to forget?

I know why you thought of killing me.

Why do you ask then?

I want to hear you say it.

Are you alone, Lucie?

You can see.

I can see nothing in the dark.

Admit the truth to me and you'll see.

Yes, I thought of killing you the night you dressed up.

I heard her get out of the bed and the floorboards creaked under her feet.

Have you been to see the man who did kill you?

It doesn't interest me.

You said you could never forgive the thief.

I've changed my mind. I don't need my savings now. Why did you think of killing me?

You were going to force me to marry you.

Force you! Force you! What with?

Then she went.

The room smelt of boar. Otherwise there was no sign that she had been there.

The thirteenth of December was her name day, *Sainte Lucie.* According to the old calendar—I read this in an almanac—Saint Lucie's day used to be the twenty-third, just after the winter solstice.

> *From the day of Saint Lucie*
> *the days lengthen by a flea's width.*

On neither the thirteenth nor on the twenty-third of December did she come back. The days grew longer.

At last the weather turned warm. My circulation improved. The old man's blood responding a little to the sun. The apple trees blossomed, the potatoes were planted, the cows were put out in the pastures. The hay was cut. One evening when the valley, full of clouds and torn mists, had its look of being the laundry of the damned, I told myself: on the next fine day I will climb up to Nîmes and pick some blueberries.

The sky was clear, and its peacefulness extended further than the furthest range of snow-capped mountains. The blueberries grow above the tree line, usually on slopes facing east or west. The southern slopes have too much sun. My mother used to dry whole sprigs of blueberries with their leaves to give to the cows when they had diarrhoea.

From the slope where I began picking, I could see the Cabrol chalet, a little to the right and below. The chalet will scarcely outlast me, I said to myself. It must be years since Henri or Edmond have done anything to it. Instead of bringing their cows up, they rent extra pasture below. There are holes in the roof and many of the shingles need replacing. The snow will be driven in, the beams will rot and one day one end of the timberwork will fall. The following winter it will look like a shipwreck; the wind, the snow, the slope, the summer sun, which burns the wood black, wear away the timber just as the sea and waves do.

The Cocadrille used a comb to pick her blueberries. When we were young, the comb didn't exist. It is like a bear's paw, made of wood and nails. It scoops up berries between each claw, and working with it is ten times as fast as picking each berry separately between finger and thumb. It collects indiscriminately: anything that passes between its nails, it keeps in its wooden paw. As well as ripe berries, you find green ones, leaves, the ends of twigs, tiny white snails and the pods of flowers. Later, to separate them, you set up a plank at an angle to the ground, wet the plank with water, take a handful of fruit from the bucket and pour them so that they roll down the wet plank; the ripe fruit roll to the bottom into the pan, and most of the leaves and the twigs and the grass and the snails stick to the wood.

The Cocadrille set up her plank on the ledge of ground behind the roadmender's house. It is a tedious operation if you are alone. You need one person to roll the fruit, and another to check in the pan below and take out the green ones which didn't stick to the wood. She must have rolled a few handfuls and then gone to squat by the pan on the ground, then rolled a few more, then gone to squat by the pan and so on.

Bent forward towards the slope, my face close to the ground, I could see the grasshoppers. There were a couple mating. Their bodies are bright green with streaks of white yellow. They are about three centimetres long, and the noise they make consists of three soft chuffs and then a long drawn-out hiss like a snake.

Tchee tchee hissssss.

When she rolled the blueberries down the wet plank, she must have heard the roar of the Jalent at the bottom of the ravine and the tinkle of the blueberries as they fell into the pan.

When blueberries are wet they darken to the colour of ink. Warm and dry in the sun they almost have a bloom like grapes. As you comb, you notice others a little higher up or a little to the side, and so you move towards them to comb them too with the bear's paw, and they in turn lead you to others and the others to others. Picking blueberries is like grazing.

As she sorted the fruit she must sometimes have gazed at the orchards and fields on the other side of the ravine, a reminder of all she had lost in her second life.

My bucket was half full. I had climbed out of sight of the place where I had begun.

Jean!

I wasn't convinced that I had heard her.

How many have you picked?

Half a bucket.

As slow as ever! she mocked.

I have calluses under my chin, I shouted, because all my life I have rested it on the handle of a shovel.

I thought this made her laugh. I could not be sure because there was a jackdaw flying overhead. And the laugh I heard might have been his cry: Drru krrie kriee! Drru krrie kriee!

Shall I help you pick?

If you wish.

I went on picking, and I heard no more, only the grasshoppers, the jackdaw, and occasionally very distantly, when the wind blew, the sound of cowbells.

I learnt what the cowbells said as a boy:

It's mine! It's mine! Can it go on? Can it go on? It can't! It can't!

I combed with the bear's paw, following the trail of the berries, grazing higher and higher. The next time I emptied the paw into the bucket, I had the impression that the level of the fruit had mounted twice as fast as before.

I straightened my back and, for the first time since her death, I saw her. She was combing, leaning against the green slope, with her head above the skyline, silhouetted against the blue sky. A scarf was tied round her head. As I watched, she climbed and went over the skyline.

She's as easy to lose as a button, La Mélanie said.

I left my bucket and climbed up to the crest. She lay there on the other side as if dead. She lay there on the soft turf between the rhododendron bushes whose flowers were finished, and she wore a scarf round her head, a crumpled black dress, socks and boots. Her shins were bare and scratched. Her eyes were shut and her arms were crossed exactly as if she were dead. It is strange I thought that, for I knew she was dead. I had seen her coffin lowered into the earth. Now there was no coffin lid, no earth, nothing but the blue sky above her.

Without thinking I took off my beret and stood there holding it in my clasped hands as I gazed down at her. Her face was grey like the outcrops of limestone. She was as motionless as a boulder. I know that it is easy in the mountains to see things that others cannot see. And then I noticed the fingers of her hands. They were stained an inky blue-black. They were like any of our fingers in André Masson's class. This was proof that she had indeed been picking blueberries this morning. In September when she was murdered there were no blueberries.

Can you see me now? I heard her say this, although her lips didn't move.

Without answering, I lay down beside her and gazed up into the sky. The sky was benign and the jackdaws were still circling in wide circles above us.

How old am I? she asked.

You were in the class of 1920. That makes you sixty-eight. No, sixty-seven.

I was born in the morning. My father was milking in the stable. White cloud like smoke was blowing through the door. My mother had her sister and a neighbour with her. I was born very quickly. The neighbour held me up feet first and cried, It's a girl. Give her to me, my mother said and then she screamed, Jesus forgive me, she screamed, she is marked with the mark of the craving, Jesus! I have marked her with the mark of the craving. Mélanie, said the neighbour, be calm. It is not the mark of the craving.

You know everything about your life now, I said.

If I told you all that I know it would take sixty-seven years.

I turned my head towards her, she was smiling at me, her blue eyes open, dirt smudged on her cheek, a few black hairs escaping from her scarf; she had the face of the Cocadrille at twenty. I moved my arm away from my body to find her hand. When I touched it, I remembered.

She led me by the hand towards the side of the mountain. Crossing an outcrop of rock she stopped, and pointed with the toe of her boot.

Cherry stones in the bird shit! She laughed. They fly with them all the way up here.

I did not recognise the path we took. At first I blamed my memory. Forty-six years is a long time. Soon I doubted whether it was a path at all. The going became steeper and steeper, and we had to push our way through pine trees which grew so close together that no sunlight ever reached the ground. There were centuries of pine needles and my boots sunk into them up to the ankles. I could feel them working their way through the wool of my socks. The needles were either ashen grey or black, they had no more colour than the lower branches of the trees. To prevent ourselves slipping we held on to the branches like ropes.

She led the way and I followed. At one point the slope was so steep that it was like climbing down the trunk of the tree itself. I suddenly remembered the porcelain chamois on her mantelpiece. I wondered whether it was still there. At least three men had fallen to their deaths whilst hunting chamois on this mountain. I hoped that she knew exactly where we were going. I doubted whether I would be capable of climbing up again. My legs were already shaking out of weakness. When I was twelve, Sylvestre, an old man, was trapped on the mountainside. He could neither climb up nor continue down. The alarm was given just before nightfall. Twenty of us with lamps set out to try to find him. If the Cocadrille disappeared, I would be like Sylvestre.

When the Devil grows old, she shouted back at me, he becomes a hermit!

Sylvestre was dead when we found him.

Fortunately she knew the path as she knew all paths. There was not a slope or crag or stream on this mountainside that she did not know. We emerged from the trees into the sunlight. We were at the top of a long bank of grass on which the paths the cows had traced over generations were like steps for us to walk down. A man in Montreal who worked for the radio once sent me a postcard of an ancient Roman theatre. The steps down the grass were like the seats of that theatre. At the bottom was a large pasture bordered by a forest. In front of the forest I could see men working.

Descending the grass steps I suddenly felt as carefree as I did before I was fully grown. Opposite Saint Lucie beside the shortest day, there is Saint Audrey beside the longest. You put on a clean shirt, newly ironed by your mother—it touches your shoulders like the face of a flat iron gone cold—you comb your hair and look at yourself in the mirror, what you see is a sixteen-year-old to whom anything may happen this Sunday. You join friends walking down to the village. You wait in the square. Everything which occurs is part of a preparation. You drink in the café. You read the signs of the future—so many of them are jokes—and yet you remain ignorant. This ignorance makes the time easy and long. You walk to the next village. There is a fight. You notice the consequences of your smallest actions and these consequences never reinforce each other. You walk back by moonlight. The girls flounce their skirts. Almost everything talked about has not yet happened. Father is asleep, beneath the smoked sausages hanging from the ceiling. You fold your trousers with care, scratch your balls and fall asleep. Sunday follows Sunday, season follows season and you go from tree to tree: there is as yet no forest. Then a day comes when there is only a forest and you have to live in it for ever: then all the days, both summer or winter, are short. I never expected to emerge from that forest, yet there I was, walking down the grass steps as if my life lay before me.

I first singled you out at school, said the Cocadrille, you made less noise than the other boys and you were methodical. You always carried a knife in your hands, always carving a stick. Once you cut yourself, and I saw you peeing over your cut to disinfect it.

Amongst the flowers in the grass there were red campions. Their pink is like the pink of paper flags all over the world when there is a fiesta.

Where are we?

This is where I am going to build.

Who does it belong to?

Me.

You!

The dead own everything, she said.

So you have land now.

Land but no seasons.

How do you plant?

We don't, we have no reason to, we have access to all the granaries in the world, they are all full.

And when they are empty?

They are full for ever.

Why don't you give potatoes to the hungry then?

We can't.

You could smuggle some across.

I chose a smoked ham for you last winter, it weighed seven kilos and was beautifully dry, I stood by when it was being smoked for two days, I was there when Emile cut the juniper bushes and when he threw water on the burning branches to make more smoke, six weeks earlier I led the pig to have her throat cut, I put my hands over her eyes so she became calm when the life flowed out of her, I gave her to the sow to suckle the day she was born, and I carried the ham to your house and I hung it in the cellar, wrapped in muslin, and when you found it two days later it was a bone, even the string had rotted and you found it in the earth in which you bury your white beet so they stay white on the cellar floor.

That bone! I muttered.

And you said: It could be the ham of a pig we killed when I was a child. I heard you say that and I knew then I could give you nothing.

You are lying.

You didn't say that and you didn't throw it over the wall?

Yes I did.

She shrugged her shoulders.

The figures I had seen from afar were working on timber, hammering nails into the joints of three vast frames which lay flat on the ground and which, when raised, would hold the walls and roof of a chalet. Each frame had five vertical columns, each column as thick as a sixty-year-old tree and twelve metres high.

They felled the trees last September, the Cocadrille said, on the day I was killed with the axe. The sap was rising.

The frames laid out on the ground were the colour of stripped radiant pine. One of the men who was hammering straightened his back. It was Marius Cabrol. I had seen him last on his deathbed. I had made the sign of the cross with a sprig of boxwood dipped in holy water over his heart. It was his daughter who had laid him out and dressed him. The way he now greeted us disconcerted me for he gave no sign that he remembered or recognised any of this. He grinned as if we had just drunk a glass together.

Fifteen spruces for the columns, he said, a dozen for the purlins, forty twenty-year-old trees for the rafters, I forget how many for the planks. We cut them all down when the axe entered her head. She told us afterwards she heard us sawing in the forest.

The first thing I did, wasn't it, was to bring you all cider and cheese and bread. I knew exactly where you were.

We were getting hungry, said Marius, smiling.

She took my hand and we stepped over the columns of the nearest frame. She was a young woman leading an old man. The men sat astride the frame as they hammered, the nails were big and they launched them into the wood with blows from the shoulder.

All right, Lucie? The hammerer who shouted this with virile impertinence was Armand who had been carried away by the Jalent and drowned. Next to him hammered Gustave who had fallen from the mountain. Georges, who hanged himself because he knew that he would become a pauper, was sewing paper flowers to the branches of a tiny spruce; the flowers were white like silver and yellow like gold. Adelin, who was killed by a tree in the forest, was tying a rope. Mathieu who was struck dead by lightning was measuring with a yellow ruler. Then I recognised Michel who died of internal bleeding after being kicked by a horse, and I saw Joset who was lost in an avalanche.

Why are they all here? I demanded.

They have come to help us, each of them brought food and drink for the meal tonight, they are good neighbours.

Why only—

Only what, Jean?

The ones who died violently.

They are the first you see.

And those who died peacefully?

There are not so many who die in their beds. It's a poor country.

Why first—? My fears that I had been led into a trap were increased.

Bend down.

She kissed me on the cheek and my fears became ridiculous. Her mouth was full of white teeth and she smelt of grass. Was it really she who fifty years ago nobody in their right mind would have thought of marrying?

They all say your trouble was that you were fearless.

I knew what I wanted.

She laughed. Between the buttons of her shirt I could make out the slight, barely noticeable rise of her breasts. Like two leaves on the earth.

Do you know, it took me no longer to learn my way around here among the dead than it took me to learn my way around the city of B. . . .

As she said this, her voice aged and became hoarser. I glanced at her. She was an old woman with a sack on her back and she looked mad.

Who is going to live in the chalet?

Somebody from behind pushed my beret over my eyes. It was Marius, her father. Once again he was grinning.

You are warmer in bed with a wife. The whole war I thought of nothing else, I thought only of caressing Mélanie in bed. The way Marius spoke had the unctuousness of a caress. There were some who had intercourse with donkeys, it never interested me, a beast isn't soft enough, when at last I came home I took her to bed and we had our fourth child. Even when I was old and lost my warmth, I thought of going to bed when I was working alone in the fields, sometimes thinking about it made me warm. There are those who call me lazy. It was my idea of happiness, you'll see for yourself, if you don't see now—it's better than sleeping alone.

The Cocadrille walked away, across her back was tied the blue umbrella and over her shoulder she carried a sack.

Aren't you forgetting that your daughter has been a spinster all her life? I asked.

Ah! my poor Jean, my poor future son-in-law, it's now that she's at the marrying age. Why else would I be building a chalet for her?

You were never a carpenter, I pointed out, and sixty-eight is no marrying age!

We can become anything. That is why injustice is impossible here. There may be the accident of birth, there is no accident of death. Nothing forces us to remain what we were. The Cocadrille could be seventeen, tall, with wide hips and with breasts you couldn't take your eyes off—only then you wouldn't know her, would you?

Once more I had the feeling of not yet having entered the forest, of all my life being in front of me.

All the men you see working here, whispered Marius—I remembered the milk running off her breasts—have married her!

Not Georges! I exclaimed.

Georges was the first. He married her the day after her funeral. The bridesmaids took the flowers from the grave. Those who die violently fall into each other's arms.

Am I to die violently? I asked.

Do you want to marry her? His smile had now become a leer.

Everything's ready! a man shouted.

The frame lay on the ground, constructed, finished, waiting to be lifted up into the air. To lift such a frame, thirty-five or forty men are needed. They came from every direction. All those whom I recognised were among the dead. Some carried ladders. Some were speaking and joking to one another and I could not hear their words. All of them greeted Marius à Brine who stood beside the sablière, which is the horizontal timber on the ground into which the frame, when vertical, has to be fitted. He who was no carpenter had become the master builder.

The wood of the frame smelt strongly of pine resin. Mixed with wax, this resin makes a good poultice for the cure of sciatica, a complaint from which many of us suffer as a result of carrying heavy loads on the slopes. We bent down together to lift the frame with our hands.

Marius was shouting so that everyone lifted at the same moment.

Tchee! Tchee! Lift!

And again. Tchee! Tchee! Hissssss!

The dead got their forearms under the frame. Bent double over the ground, they cradled the wood as you cradle a baby.

Tchee! Tchee! Hissssss!

Wood is to us what iron has been to others for two thousand years. We even made gearwheels out of wood.

With each heave we raised the frame a little higher. We could just rest our forearms on our thighs. The dead who were lifting the king-post, the vertical beam which holds the point of the roof, were now able to slip their shoulders under it, bundling together like bearers carrying a coffin.

When the frame was too high for us to lift with our hands, we thrust with poles. There was a pole tied to each column. Half a dozen or so men gathered around each pole, thrusting it up, their grasping hands overlapping. Ten hands, fifty fingers, they were indistinguishable one from the other except where there was a scarred severed finger. How many of our fingers have been cut off by saws! Yet better a finger than a life, the living had a habit of saying.

With each thrust we grunted. The grunts came from the pit of the stomach. Sometimes a dead man farted with the effort. The Cocadrille had come back and was standing by my side, the same scarf round her head, white hairs straggling out of it.

Why do you want a hayloft, you have no land? I gasped.

Tchee! Tchee! Hissssss!

The gigantic frame which was going to span three rooms, a stable and a hayloft—a hayloft such as a hundred haycarts, pulled across the wooden floor by the mares, would scarcely fill—shook with each heave. Or, rather, it was we who shook.

To store our hay, she said.

You have no cows.

To have thirty-five litres of milk a day for butter and cheese.

Tchee! Tchee! Hissssss!

You don't need to eat, I said.

To support ourselves and to have something to hand on to our children! She smiled, as she had when she handed me the butter fifty years before.

The faces of the dead were red with the effort of grasping, heaving and holding, their mouths were strained, their eyes bulged, the muscles and veins on their necks stood out like ropes and cords beneath the skin.

I was always told the dead rest after a lifetime's work, I muttered.

When they remember their past, they work, she said. What else should they remember?

The shoulders of those who had taken off their shirts glistened with sweat, yet the frame was still below the angle of forty-five degrees.

Again! Tchee! Tchee! Lift!

The gigantic naked frame scarcely stirred. It was as if another forty men were pushing it down against us.

We need more help, go and fetch some others, round up the neighbours!

Jésus, Marie and Joseph!

A ménage à trois!

Be quick about it!

The Cocadrille ran towards the forest. It was not possible to lay the frame down on the ground. It is easier to raise such a weight than to lower it, and in lowering it there is the risk of somebody being trapped beneath it. Pierre, who was on the next pole, had been trapped under a frame, with both his legs broken, and had died two years later.

No man should suffer the same thing twice.

We were able to prop several poles against the ground. We wedged in several ladders. Most of the weight was taken off us, yet nobody took their hands off the poles. The great frame pointed into the sky, not into the dark blue sky above us, it pointed towards the pale sky beyond the distant mountains. A jackdaw—I cannot say whether he was the same one—was circling above the frame. At one moment I thought he was going to alight on it. Everything was still, none of the dead was moving.

When the Cocadrille came back from the forest, she was young; several men followed her. As so many years before, I was astounded by how fast she ran.

Yes, I should have married her! I said it out loud. The dead were lost in their own thoughts. Nobody responded.

The newcomers joined the groups round each pole.

Tchee! Tchee! Hissssss!

The frame shifted up five or six degrees. Together we were going to master it. As soon as it passed the half-way mark of forty-five degrees it would become easier.

As a precautionary measure some men were already holding the ropes in case the almost vertical frame should incline too far and fall inwards. When the frame was vertical its tusk tenons had to be slotted into the mortices of the *sablière*. Human geometry had to replace the original strength of the trees. The tusks entered the mouths of the *sablière*, all five at almost the same moment.

I will marry you, I said, turning towards her.

To my horror 'Mile à Lapraz was standing beside her. He was flushed and looked as if he had been drinking. I had seen him only a week before in the village. It occurred to me then that all the men she had brought back running with her were among the living.

You will be a witness, she said to 'Mile.

Where are we? I mumbled. Aren't we far from the village?

We are outside the church, Jean, where the men stand at funerals and the newly married are photographed.

My face must have shown my consternation.

He's so careful, slurred 'Mile à Lapraz, nodding in my direction, he wipes his arse before he has shat!

You should talk, the Cocadrille snapped back at him. You've lived alone all your life, you get drunk alone, your bed smells like a distillery. Jean has been to the other side of the world, he married, he had children, he came back, he picks blueberries very slowly, all right he pretends to be deaf, he wanted to kill me, he has taken his time, but now at the last moment, the very last moment, he has agreed to marry me, you would never have the spunk to do that, 'Mile.

Now that the first frame was in place, she went from man to man with a bottle and a glass offering them to drink.

After we had rested, Marius à Brine called us to start raising the second frame. Encouraged by the sight of the first, upright, its columns as thick as trees, its white wood framing triangles of deep blue sky, we lifted the second frame, call by call:

Tchee! Tchee! Hissssss!

We lifted it without stopping, and the tusks of its columns entered the mouths of the *sablière*. We raised the third frame even quicker than the second. Some said this was because the wood was less green and so lighter.

Fifty men stood looking up at the three frames which indicated the full dimensions of the chalet; it was an outline drawing in white on the green pasture, the dark forest, and the blue sky.

No one will kill themselves in this chalet, she said.

The men whom the Cocadrille had brought from the village announced that, if they were no longer needed, they would return.

Marius à Brine did his best to persuade them to stay for the feast they would have as soon as the work was over. They said they must go.

Come back later, insisted Marius, come back with your women for the feast!

The villagers were noncommittal.

Several of the dead came over to thank them. At least let us pay you another glass, they said.

No need to thank us, answered the living, you'd do the same for us.

That goes without saying, whenever a house is built some of us are there.

I watched the villagers walk away into the forest. Gradually they formed a single file, each one walking by himself. Their going disturbed me: I was alone again with the dead. At the same time I was relieved by their going; I would have no questions to answer. What language do they speak in Buenos Aires? How long have you been a widower? Are you really thinking of remarrying? How did she persuade you?

The work which remained to be done was now more divided and less anxious. We had to lift the purlins, the beams which run the length of the roof, into their positions, fit their joints and nail them. Every purlin was numbered with a numeral, written as André Masson had taught us all at school, and every joint was indicated twice on each piece of wood, with a capital letter. Some of the dead were on ladders and some worked on the ground. They made more comments than before and more jokes. Those on the ground fixed temporary bars at an angle to the future walls, like buttresses. Along these they pushed and pulled the purlins up with ropes.

The first to be fixed in place was the lowest, the timber bordering the overhanging roof. Against the wall beneath this overhanging roof, the wood for the stove would be stacked, sheltered from the snow and the rain. Against the southern wall protected by the roof she'd plant lettuces and parsley, and, along the edge of the same bed, multi-coloured pansies, which have the colours of most of the precious stones in the world. Under the roof behind the first purlin, sparrows would nest and on the posts of the fence, for which the stakes have not yet been cut or pointed, a pair of crows would sit, waiting for her to come out to feed the chickens. I heard her calling them.

She took my hand in her stiff, calloused, grabbing, picking, old woman's hand. It was no longer possible for me to think of her as young.

There is no need for you to work, she said, they have enough help, we can sit in the sun.

And the food? I asked. Is everything prepared?

Everything.

I don't see any tables or benches.

They are in the church, it'll only take a minute to bring them out.

At her funeral when people were still filing out of the cemetery, the Mayor told the local veterinary surgeon: And so we gave her the roadmender's house, it was the best we could think of. You have to reckon with the fact that if she'd lived in a city, she would certainly have been put in an institution many years ago . . .

Look! she said, tapping my shoulder, they will soon be finished.

We were sitting there side by side, watching the mountains, and the men working. We were the eldest, all the working dead were younger than us. The Cocadrille's features and the backs of my own hands were a reminder of our age. The Cocadrille was sixty-seven when she was murdered, and I was three years older.

So, my contraband, I've smuggled you here, she said. An unlit cigarette was stuck to her lower lip which protruded and was blueish from the blueberries she had eaten.

The feeling of endless promise such as I hadn't experienced since I was young bore me up, cradled me. I saw my father making rabbit hutches, and myself handing him the nails. I must have been eleven the year when, under my mother's careful supervision, I bled and skinned my first rabbit. At the catechism class the Cocadrille knew by heart the answers I could not remember.

What is avarice?

Avarice is an excessive longing for the good things of life and particularly money.

Is love of the good things of life ever justified?

Yes, there is a justified love of the good things of life and this love inspires foresight and thrift.

On feast days in the Argentine the peones killed and ate turkeys: emigration offered me no new promises. The promise of the Place d'Etoile and the promise of the Arenne Corrientes in Buenos Aires were simply revivals of what I had already hoped in the village. I couldn't have imagined those places from the village, yet I did imagine my pleasure, the same pleasure they promised and didn't give me.

Pleasure is always your own, and it varies as much and no more than pain does. I had become accustomed to pain, and now to my surprise the hope of pleasure, the hope I had known when I was eleven, was coming from the old woman with the unlit cigarette who called me her contraband. Where had my life gone? I asked myself.

The dead were nailing the rafters. By the time all forty were in place, the sun was low and the bars of the roof cast a shadow on the grass beside the chalet which looked like a dark cage. The bars were the shadows.

Do you want to nail the bouquet? shouted Marius à Brine.

She waited for me to answer. I could feel her gaze through her half-shut eyes. The force of my reply surprised me.

From the corner of each of her puckered, squeezed eyes a tear came like juice. She crossed her arms to grasp her flat chest with her stiff hands. Her mouth stretched in a smile. Her tears ran down the deep lines to the corners of her mouth and she licked her upper lip.

Go, she said to me.

Marius handed me the hammer and the nails and I walked over to the foot of the first ladder. There was Georges, who hanged himself because he knew he was to become a pauper and would be sent in the winter to the old people's hostel where half the inmates were incoherent. The money to build this hostel had been donated by a rich engineer from the region who had built many bridges for roads and railways far away. Georges planned his suicide as carefully as the engineer planned his bridges, he fixed a hooked wire to a tall wooden pole, ran the wire down it and with the help of this pole touched a high-tension wire, near the centre of the village, in a place where he would disturb no one. At the instant he died, all the lights in the village went out. Now Georges handed me the spruce to which he had attached the yellow and white paper flowers shaped like roses. With this bouquet across my shoulder, like a sweep's brush, I climbed the ladder, which Georges held for me.

At the top a man I did not know was sitting on a cross beam. He put out his hand to steady me as I stepped off the ladder. I shook my head. It was a long time since I'd been on a roof and I needed no help. Like all of us I was born to it. Why were so many of us obliged to go to Paris as chimney sweeps? We lived on a roof; almost the first steps we take are on slopes as steep as our roofs. As long as I can climb up a ladder and lift one foot above the next, I need no help.

Who are you? I asked, you're not from here.

Lucie knew me as Saint-Just, he replied.

You were in the Maquis!

We were ordered to dig our graves and we were shot.

I will tell you something, I said. There were Nazis who escaped after the Liberation and came to the Argentine, they changed their names and they lived off the fat of the pampas.

They only escaped for a moment.

You can't be so sure, can you?

Justice will be done.

When?

When the living know what the dead suffered.

He said this without a trace of bitterness in his voice, as if he had more than all the patience in the world.

I climbed a second ladder with the tree across my shoulder, and sat astride the roof. There was a slight breeze; I felt it on my forearms. I could see the trees in the forest. In the east the snow on the mountains was turning a very diluted rose, no redder than the water of a stream when an animal has been killed. I looked down through the open roof into the upturned faces of the dead who had assembled to watch what I was going to do.

It was then that I noticed the band. They were standing at the end of the chalet, by the first frame. They were like the band I had joined as a drummer when I was fourteen. The band that played the soldiers out of the village. The sun was by now too low in the sky for the brass and silver instruments to dazzle. Their metals shone only dully like water in a mountain lake.

I began to make my way—not without some difficulty—along the ridge of the roof. When I reached the end, I looked down on the upturned faces; they were grinning like skulls. I lifted the tree off my shoulder and held it upright. What I had to do now was to nail it to the king-post. Suddenly from behind two thin arms clasped me round the ribs.

Hold the tree, I said.

She couldn't reach it.

I'll sit on your shoulders, she said.

The onlookers below started to cheer. All the remembered dead of the village were there, women and children as well as men. She held the tree and I drove in four nails.

The little tree pointed up into the sky. She sat behind me, her arms relaxed. We were like a couple riding on their horse going to work in the fields. Her hands lay in my lap.

The bandsmen raised the instruments to their mouths, the drummers lifted their sticks. For a moment they remained transfixed and still, then they started to play.

The sign of the tree nailed to the roof was in honour of a work completed. All that remained to be done was to cover the roof with *bûchilles* cut from the beams, to lay the floors, nail boards on the walls, make and fit the doors and windows, construct the chimney, build the cupboards, make the shelf for the bed. It was the work of months. Yet the whole weight-bearing frame which promised shelter was there.

How can I tell you what the band played. I could hum the melody and you would not hear it. The bandsmen were dead and they played the music of silence. On Ascension Day the village band goes out into the country across the slopes, between the orchards, and, wherever there are two or three farms, it stops to play. Three summers I went out with them as drummer before I had to leave to find work. The music drowns the noise of the water in the *bassin*, it drowns the streams, it drowns the cuckoo. At each farm they gave us cider or *gnôle* to drink. The saxophonist, who played like a bird, always got drunk. Sweating under our peaked caps and in our brass-buttoned jackets we played as well and as loudly as we knew how, and the louder we played, the more still became the mountains and the trees of the forest. Only the deaf butterflies continued to flutter and climb, close and open their wings. On Ascension Day we played to the dead, and the dead, behind the motionless mountains and the still trees, listened to us. Now everything was the other way round, it was the dead who played at the foot of the chalet, and I, astride the roof, who was listening.

The village began to dance to the music, on the grass under the roof timbers. The Cocadrille beat her hands on my thighs to the rhythm of the music. I saw that my blood had not turned as cold with age as I thought it had. When the music stopped she kept her hands there.

The band started up again.

Wait for me, she whispered.

Climbing to her feet, she walked along the ridge of the roof like a chamois. As she went down I prided myself on having learnt from experience. Her return would be startling and unexpected. Still aroused, I tried to foresee how she would come back: perhaps she would come back aged twenty and naked as though she had been bathing in a river.

It was impossible to make out the uniforms of the bandsmen. Occasionally an instrument glinted like an ember when you blow on it. They knew the dances they were playing by heart, for it was too dark to read the notes on the music cards clipped to their instruments. The dancers, as the light disappeared, packed closer and closer together into the chalet.

I peered down, looking for the Cocadrille. The darkness was not so total that the whiteness of her body would not give off a certain light, like the white flowers sewn on to the tree did.

I felt my way down the first ladder. The dancers were now packed together in the area which would be the stable, where we would milk the cows. The cows were there. One was licking the head of her neighbour. Her tongue was so strong that when she licked round the eye, it pulled it open, revealing the eyeball, as you must do if you are looking for something which has entered the eye and is hurting it.

Seeing that eye, I saw the truth. The Cocadrille was not going to come back. Or if she came back, she would come back as nothing.

Lucie! Lucie!

Beyond the timbers of the roof the stars were shining. They shine over some oceans like they shine over the alpage. They are very bright and the similarity isn't in their brightness; it is simply that their distance isn't confusing. The Milky Way was folded into the sky like the ranunculi bordering the stream are folded into the hill beside the abandoned Cabrol chalet.

I missed my footing, rolled, like a log, down a precipitous slope. What saved me were some rhododendron bushes at which I instinctively, unthinkingly, grasped. I never lost consciousness. Ten metres further down was a sheer drop of a hundred metres. I had a broken arm and shoulder. When it was light, I somehow made my way down the path where the cumin grows, my arm hanging loose like the tongue of a bell.

Ten days later I met 'Mile à Lapraz in the village.

Where were you, 'Mile, ten days ago?

At home.

Where exactly, doing what?

The Friday, you mean?

Yes, the Friday.

Wait, Friday. I remember, I was ill in bed. I had terrible pains in the stomach. A white weasel was eating it. I swear to you I thought it was the end. As it turned out, he didn't want me, and so here I am. I'll pay you a drink.

Standing by the counter of the café, he clinked glasses and said conspiratorially: To the two of us they didn't take!

Later when my arm was still in plaster, I walked up to the roadmender's house. The weight of the plaster round my arm was as heavy as iron. I climbed slowly, letting one leg follow the other:

the body becomes accustomed to a rhythm not unlike that of a cradle being slowly rocked from side to side. After an hour or two of such climbing you promise yourself a pleasure: the pleasure at night of lying absolutely still.

The hospital had discovered nothing with X-rays, yet I was convinced that at least one of my ribs was fractured. With each breath it stabbed me on the left-hand side, near the heart. I stopped once and looked down at the valley and the road that led away. I remembered the Cocadrille's story of the curé climbing up to the house and being taken ill. What was it that he muttered when she loosened his clothes on the table?

I had not been to the Cocadrille's house since the night when she came down from the loft wearing her wedding veil. The chicken hutches had been taken away from the ledge, and the door was ajar. I knocked. I could hear only the Jalent below. I pushed the door open. The table and chair were still there. There was nothing on the mantelpiece. Who had taken the plates? I opened the stove. It was stuffed with the recent remains of a picnic. On the wall by the cupboard some initials had been scratched, neither hers nor mine, and beside them was a drawn heart, the shape of an owl's face, with an arrow through it.

In the stable I found some sacks and the bear's paw. There was no sign of the blue umbrella. I climbed up the ladder to the loft. She dreamt about that ladder. She was in her bed in the loft and a young man climbed up and started to undress to get into bed with her. She could see that he was beautiful. He slipped between the blankets beside her and just as she felt his warmth, she woke up. The bed too had gone.

Before I was six, before I looked after the cows, perhaps I was only two or three, I used to watch my father in the kitchen on winter mornings, when it was still as dark as night. He knelt by an iron beast, feeding it. If I came near, he shouted at me. He knelt down at one side of the animal, between its iron legs and, breathing deeply, he whispered to it. I saw my father praying in church. In the kitchen he prayed in long breaths, blowing and sighing. I never saw the iron animal's face, which was inside its stomach. After a while I could feel the warmth filling the kitchen, and my father would sit beside the animal, warming his feet between its legs, before putting his boots on and going to feed the other animals. Now when I light the stove in the morning, I say to myself: I and the fire are the only living things in this house; my father, mother, brothers, the horse, cows, rabbits, chickens, all have gone. And the Cocadrille is dead.

I say that, and I do not altogether believe it. Sometimes it seems to me that I am nearing the edge of the forest. I will never again be sixteen; if I am to leave the forest, it will be on the far side. Do I feel this because I am old and tired? I doubt it. The old animal when he feels his strength disappearing hides himself in the very centre of the forest, he does not dream of leaving it. Is it a longing for death such as an animal never feels? Is it only death that will at last deliver me from the forest? There are moments when I see something different, moments when a blue sky reminds me of Lucie Cabrol. At these moments I see again the roof which we raised, built with the trees, and then I am convinced that it is with the love of the Cocadrille that I shall leave the forest.

Potatoes

The cock crows
  the soil its black feather spread
    claws its stone
      and lays its eggs

Don't lift them too soon
  they give light off
    through their moon skin
     to the dead

During the snow
  heaped in cellars
    they gravely offer
     body to the soup

When they fail
  the plough has no meat
    and men starve like the great bear
     in the winter night

Acknowledgements

The trilogy *Into Their Labours* has occupied me during the last fifteen years. During this period, Tom Engelhardt has edited my books. Dear Tom, you have encouraged, corrected, and upheld me. Thank you.

Perhaps I would never have had the courage to begin the project if I had not received, before a page was written and until today, the support of the Transnational Institute in Amsterdam. To everyone in Paulus Potterstraat and Connecticut Avenue and to Saul Landau, thank you.